Outta Here

Lea Beddia

James Lorimer & Company Ltd.,
Publishers, Toronto

James Lorimer & Company Ltd., Publishers acknowledges funding support from the Ontario Arts Council (OAC), an agency of the Government of Ontario. We acknowledge the support of the Canada Council for the Arts, which last year invested $153 million to bring the arts to Canadians throughout the country. This project has been made possible in part by the Government of Canada and with the support of Ontario Creates.

Cover design: Tyler Cleroux
Cover image: Shutterstock

Library and Archives Canada Cataloguing in Publication
Title: Outta here / Lea Beddia.
Names: Beddia, Lea, author.
Identifiers: Canadiana (print) 20230228534 | Canadiana (ebook) 20230228542
  | ISBN 9781459417304 (hardcover) | ISBN 9781459417298 (softcover)
  | ISBN 9781459417311 (EPUB)
Classification: LCC PS8603.E42435 O98 2023 | DDC jC813/.6—dc23

Published by:
James Lorimer & Company
Ltd., Publishers
117 Peter Street, Suite 304
Toronto, ON, Canada
M5V 0M3
www.lorimer.ca

Distributed in Canada by:
Formac Lorimer Books
5502 Atlantic Street
Halifax, NS, Canada
B3H 1G4

Distributed in the US by:
Lerner Publisher Services
241 1st Ave. N.
Minneapolis, MN, USA
55401
www.lernerbooks.com

Printed and bound in the United States

Table of Contents

For Mom and Dad, with all my love

From the Author...

Addiction can change a person's behaviour and relationships. It can be shocking and traumatic. You may or may not have family and friends that have been affected by it, but if you do, you already know about the ways it can change people. If you don't, this story may help you understand.

Before you read on, I want you to know that the story I'm telling in this book involves abuse, trauma, and violence toward animals. But I would also like you to know that this is really a story about a young woman who succeeds in finding her way out of very tough family circumstances.

This book is also about resilience, which I've learned from the almost two thousand students I've taught so far. But this isn't one particular person's story. This is a piece of fiction and not meant to glamorize or expose anyone's hardships.

I wrote this book out of compassion and empathy. So many kids are struggling. Pre- or post-pandemic, their lives are sometimes secret from what they show. We need to bring that out into the light.

If you or someone you care about is suffering from abuse or drug addiction, please contact social services in your area. Talk to an adult who cares for you. Tell them. And if they don't hear you, tell them again. Or seek out someone else who will hear what you are saying.

My inspiration for this novel came from author and speaker Ash Beckham, who said, "Hard is not relative. Hard is hard." We need to listen to each other, empathize, and lift each other up as high as our strength will allow.

And you, today's youth, are all strength.

L.B.

Chapter 1
It's No Secret

It's no secret I hate this shitty town. It's smack between a cement factory on one end and a tire factory on the other, with farmers' fields on the outskirts of it all. So, in summer and fall, it always smells like a delightful mix of cow manure and burnt rubber, with a constant haze of limestone dust in the air. This is Joliette. Home, sweet home.

I stare out the window when I should be writing my history test. The first day of spring has already passed, but a thick layer of slushy muck covers the streets, thanks to last night's snowfall. The overpass outside our classroom window connects Joliette to Montreal. The city is only about an hour away, but there's no way for me to escape. At least not until graduation. If I can convince Mom to let me go to college. She might try to convince me to stay in town, but the only college here is in French. I'd flunk out in the first week. I can barely keep my marks above a pass in French class. Just enough for me to graduate.

My phone buzzes in my back pocket and drags me out of my daydream. Must be Mom. Crap. I was supposed to put my phone on Mr. Lessard's desk before the test. If he sees me with it, I'll get a zero, and I can't afford another failing grade. I can't stay here another year.

I slide my hand in my pocket and try to turn the phone off, afraid everyone will hear it buzzing. It slips out. Bangs onto the linoleum as Mr. Lessard is circulating around the room. He picks it up, looks at the screen, and carries it to his desk. He doesn't say a word, just sits back down, scratching his well-trimmed beard. I'm dead. I try to focus on my test. Jacques Cartier and his voyages to New France. Champlain and the founding of Quebec City. But the dates and details jumble in my head. I shade in Champlain's moustache and goatee on my doodle instead. Trucks rumble across the overpass.

The dates of Cartier's voyages come back to me: 1534, 1535, 1541. The founding of Quebec City, 1608. I scribble them down. Drawing always helps me clear my mind. It's like once my pen moves to start drawing, my ideas can glide into words. Mr. Lessard is the only teacher who doesn't mind me doodling on my work. He likes my cartoons of historical figures. He even cut one out from one of my essays and stuck it on his bulletin board: John A. Macdonald, the first prime minister of Canada, with droopy eyelids and a groggy look on his face. He has a mug of beer in one hand and a document on the creation of residential schools in the other. Mr. Lessard said it was more accurate than any other drawing he'd seen of the prime minister. He said I could have a career as a political cartoonist. I found that funny because politics are not my thing, but I'm glad he liked it.

He passes by my desk again and taps a finger on my doodles.

"Nice," he whispers. "We'll talk after class."

Perfect. I look up at him. He has wrinkles like V's around his eyes. He's smiling, but if he thinks I was cheating with my phone, I'm done.

The bell rings and everyone walks out. None of my friends take this class. This is a Grade Ten class and I'm in eleventh, but if I want to graduate, I need to repeat this course. And graduating is my only chance onto the overpass and out of this place. At least in Quebec we finish high school earlier than in other provinces. Otherwise, I'd be stuck here another year. At the same time, leaving and living in the city is more than a little scary.

With everyone gone, Mr. Lessard collects my test and gives back my phone.

"I think you got a message," he says.

"I'm so sorry. I forgot to put it on your desk." He nods, waiting for me to say more. I use the Mom excuse because everyone knows about her accident. The whole class witnessed her car accident last winter when her car slid across the black ice on the overpass. She skidded into the guardrail, fractured a bunch of bones in her leg, and had emergency surgery. It's been over a year, but she still has trouble walking. "It was probably my mom. She didn't realize I had a test today. I'm so sorry."

"Okay," he says. "But the rules . . ." I deflate. I get it. Everyone heard my phone fall to the floor. Everyone saw him carry it to his desk. And everyone knows the rules.

"I don't have Wi-Fi access on my phone. So even if I wanted to cheat . . ."

"Okay. Wait while I correct your test."

"Can I eat while you do?" It's lunchtime, and I haven't had a thing to eat since last night.

"Go ahead." He sits at his desk, his red pen of doom hacking away at my test.

I grabbed a bunch of packaged croissants from the free breakfast bin this morning, but my bus arrives at school just before the final bell, with no time to eat them. I shove the first one into my mouth. There are another four in my bag. I take my time with the second one. I flip over my phone and read the message from Mom, the one Mr. Lessard probably read before giving it back to me:

Mom
S.O.S. No food in the house. Get some.

Wonderful. A (likely) failed test and an empty fridge to start the week. I open the window next to me. Trucks fly across the overpass, rumbling and vibrating. Thick black smoke blasts into the air. More smoke rises beyond the overpass from the limestone factory. The air outside will smell like dirty dampness and burnt tires. I'm desperate to pass this test.

Chapter 2
In My Dreams

"Not bad, Élise. Eighty-eight percent."

"Better than *not bad*," I say, after swallowing my last bite of croissant. I'm saving the other three for later. "What about my phone?"

"I think you have lots to worry about. I think you forgot your phone, and I think you need to answer your mom's text."

"Yeah," I say, reading my screen again.

"This time — *only* this time — I will overlook it. You've been working so hard. You're almost there. I'm not going to be the one to hold you back, but on a final exam, a ministry exam . . ." Mr. Lessard picks up the stack of tests on his desk and shuffles through them.

"I know. If I was caught with my phone, automatic zero."

"Okay. Consider yourself warned. But this is impressive." He waves my test paper in front of him, stands, and gives it to me. "Great job."

"Thanks," I say, taking the test from him.

"And as always, I love the drawings. Cartier on a speedboat. Hilarious." He turns the page. "And this one of Champlain with the apron?" He reads the caption under the drawing. "*Father of New French Toast.* It's very funny."

"Thanks. I had trouble with Champlain's face. The goatee isn't right. Too dark, I think."

"No one actually knows for sure what he looked like. He never posed for a portrait, and the artists who drew him did so from memory. For all we know, he had no facial hair." He's going off into history mode. He does this in class too. Tells stories, goes off on tangents, which is why even though I don't love the subject, Mr. Lessard is the best teacher. "Okay. You're free to go. Have a good day."

"Thanks again, Mr. Lessard. I appreciate it."

"I know you do. You're welcome." I gather my books and head out the door, but he stops me. "Oh, wait, I forgot. I'm supposed to give you this. From the guidance department, I think."

My arms get tingly and cold. Anytime the guidance counsellor has wanted to see me, it was to talk about Mom, but it's been a while. Not since last year. Not since her accident. "It's a permission form," Mr. Lessard tells me. "For the college open houses."

"Oh," I say, more relaxed.

"Any prospects yet?" he asks me. He packs the tests into his bag and zips it closed.

"I don't know. Depends on my marks, I guess."

"What's the dream?"

"I'm not sure I'll go to college." I hold my books tighter.

Mr. Lessard looks out the window. At the overpass. Can he read my mind? Does he know that structure is both my way out and my anchor?

"You deserve it."

"I deserve more school? More torture?" I joke.

"Ha. You deserve every opportunity."

"Thanks, Mr. Lessard. I'll think about it."

"Dream about it."

I probably could only attend in my dreams. I'm doomed to stay here forever.

I leave the classroom, feeling worse than when I walked in. An hour and fifteen minutes ago, all I had on my mind was a history test and lunch. Now I have my whole future and another meal to worry about.

Chapter 3
Stupid

I approach Lily at our usual corner table in the cafeteria.

"Where were you?" she asks.

"History test."

"How was it?" She unwraps a sandwich. "Ugh. Ham again." She hands it to me. "Interested?"

"Yeah. Sure." I try not to devour it like a T-Rex being handed fresh meat. "What about you?" I say. "You don't need to eat?"

"Big breakfast this morning. Pancakes. The works."

"Nice." I take another bite, imagining maple syrup and apple cinnamon pancakes, like I know Mrs. McLeod, Lily's mom, makes. She usually makes big breakfasts on weekends. Mom and I used to go over for brunch once in a while, but it's Monday. "What was the occasion?"

"The Tempest's birthday today."

"Right." *The Tempest*, Lily's pet name for her little sister, Tamara. It's accurate.

"Hey, it's your turn at the bake sale, remember?" Lily says.

"Crap," I say, my mouth full of ham sandwich. "Almost forgot." I look over at the centre of the cafeteria. Our Leadership teacher is sitting at the table where I should be, selling baked goods to raise money for the Sunny Break long-term-care facility. He'll be pissed I'm late. I approach him, trying to look apologetic.

"Sorry I'm late." He puffs up in his chair. "I was writing my history test."

"All right, Élise. This is your philanthropy project, not mine."

"I know, sir. So sorry. It ran a little late. Thanks for getting things started."

"I brought down all the cookies and muffins. Cashbox is here. I'll come pick it up at the end of the lunch period."

"Great, thanks," I say, taking his seat.

Lily pulls up a chair next to me. "Want company?"

"Yeah, please," I say, taking another bite of her sandwich.

"Did you see this?" she says, waving her copy of the field trip permission form.

"Yeah. Mr. Lessard gave me one in History."

"We're going, right?"

"A whole day away from school? I'm in."

"Think of the opportunities. We'll get to meet students who are actually in college and ask them questions about actual programs. I'm so confused reading all the information online. I'm dying to talk to someone who's living it." Lily is talking so fast I lean in to listen better so I can keep up. She's so excited her face turns red, almost as red as her hair.

"Still. Missing school will be a nice change."

"You're not even a little interested in seeing what these schools have to offer?" Of course I am. I know I want to study art or design or something creative, but going to college in the city means three things:

One, leaving this hole-in-the-wall town, which also means getting an apartment, which requires money, which I do not have.

Two, leaving Mom. Which requires guts. Also things I do not have.

Three, coming clean to Lily about my money issues, which I do not want to do.

"Of course I'm interested, but it's a lot to think about."

"Applications are due at the end of the month, so think quick."

A boy a grade younger than us approaches the table. He takes a plate and loads it with cookies and cakes, all delicious things my teammates baked for the project. He gently balances cookies on top of cakes and rice crispy treats.

"All for you?" I ask, transferring some onto a second plate so he doesn't lose it all.

"I'm buying a round for my table."

"That's six dollars," I tell him. He sets the plate down carefully and fishes through his pockets. He pulls out a chewed-up pencil, Rocket candies, and a wrinkled-up twenty-dollar bill. I dig for change in the cashbox.

"Keep it," he says.

"You don't want your change?" I ask.

"My grandpa is at the Sunny Break facility. I'm happy to donate."

"Awesome, thanks," I say. I give the twenty to Lily, and she makes note of the quantities of goods sold, then adds a column on our spreadsheet for donations. Under it she writes, *$14.* Our Leadership teacher is strict about us keeping track of everything.

"Here," Lily says, sliding over the spreadsheet. "I have to go to the art studio and finish up my nature painting." She rolls her eyes.

"Want help?" I ask.

"The teacher would know it wasn't my work. Too obvious."

"I can dim it down, color outside the lines a little if you like, to make it look like it was you."

"Hilarious. I'll see you later." She places her permission form neatly in the pocket of her agenda book and writes *sign formm* in today's box on her calendar. "Want to come over and study tonight?"

"Study? What for now?"

"Science. Next week." She flips the agenda to next week where she's written *Science Test* and circled it in pink highlighter about twelve times. "Seriously, what would you do without me?"

"Right. Sure, I can come over."

"You can have supper with us, if you like. Mom said it's fine. And there will be birthday cake."

I think of Mom, home alone, fridge empty. I think of the six bucks I have in my pocket and the groceries she wants me to pick up. "I have to stop at home first. Mom asked me to get a few things. Then I'll bike over."

"That'll take forever. Why not get off the bus with me? Mom can drive you home after studying."

Lily is organized and likes things her way.

"Lily, Mom wasn't feeling too great today. She wanted me to pick up some stuff from the corner store before heading home."

She knows my look, my tone, and enough about Mom not to argue. She knows Mom and I don't get along like we used to, that we are scraping by, but doesn't know how short we are on money. She's barely been in the apartment since the accident. "Fine," Lily says, "but promise me you'll ask her to sign the permission form tonight so we can visit colleges together." She stands and I salute. She rolls her eyes again and heads toward the art studio.

I pick up the permission form and read through it. The trip includes lunch, which is great, but there's a fee. Twenty dollars. Whatever I have in my wallet minus food for tonight is not going to cut it. Asking Mom for money is not an option. She probably has less than I do.

"Three rice crispy treats, please," a seventh grader says. I plate them for him and pop his money into the cashbox. The wrinkled twenty-dollar bill from earlier is sitting on the top. I try to picture Mom as I ask her for money. She'll look at the floor. Then at me. She'll sigh. Then get angry. Like I'm asking too much. Then she'll say no. Then she'll go on about how I'm not even eighteen and I have no business being on my own. Because being home is so much better. I picture Lily, begging me to come. I pick up the twenty-dollar bill. The old-folks' home needs a new rec room. This charity drive was my idea, but I want to go to the open house. Not for Lily, but for myself. My arms prickle with nerves, but no one is looking. I slip the money into my pocket, as the Leadership teacher walks toward me through the cafeteria. At the same time, the senior soccer team is at the table, ready to devour everything in sight, and I'm trying to count their change and plate their desserts without dropping anything. When the feeding frenzy is over, the bell rings for the end of lunch and my teacher picks up the cashbox and spreadsheet. I walk to my locker, hand in my pocket, flipping the twenty-dollar bill between my fingers — and then my whole body freezes.

The spreadsheet.

The new column Lily added for the donation.

My teacher will want to know where the money is.

I can't believe I was so stupid.

Chapter 4
Some Secrets

On the bus ride home, Lily is quiet. We can talk for hours about nothing at all, but on the bus, we sit next to each other every day and barely say a word. Normally it's a comfortable silence between us, but right now, I have a twenty-dollar secret burning a hole in one pocket. My other pocket holds the permission form, which means talking to Mom about college.

"See you later, then?" Lily asks when I stand to get off the bus.

"Yeah. Won't be long," I say. I drag my feet, like I'm carrying a backpack filled with all my problems. Soon enough, I'm going to topple backward.

"And don't forget the permission slip."

I walk off the bus and up the steps of *Le Dépanneur* corner store. The owner greets me, asks about school, my mom. Is she better? She should know. My mom comes in here almost every day for cigarettes. I hate living in a small town where everyone loves gossip. I buy some sliced cheese and a carton of six eggs. I barely have enough of my own money.

I continue up the hill to our house. My boots slosh through the wet snow as I reach our side door. The yellow paint is cracked and peeling, revealing brown and grey washed-out wood planks. It was due for painting last spring, but Mom was in no condition then to do it. I'm not sure she ever will be again. The screen door has a loose hinge, and the rusted metal creaks loudly. A wall of smoke pushes me back when I open the door. I imagine myself floating through the sea of smoke wearing one of those old-fashioned scuba masks, the round metal ones attached to a hose for the diver to breathe through. Mom's bedroom door is open. She's lying on her bed. The ashtray next to her bed is full. So is her pillbox. She's had the prescription renewed. I hold my breath so as not to breathe in the stink of her room and open her side window. She rolls over.

"You're home," she says. Her voice is like an old car struggling to get started on a winter morning. She coughs about a hundred times before she can talk again. "You get my message?"

"There's eggs for supper. Croissants and cheese for breakfast."

"That's it?"

"I didn't have any more money."

"Okay. I'll have some money tomorrow."

I flip the calendar on her bedside table, still open to January. Only three months behind. Mom's disability deposit won't be made for another week. "How?" I ask.

"I'll get some." She's groggy from the medication.

"I'm going to Lily's for supper. Stopped by to drop off the food."

"Again? They don't mind having you over so often?"

"I was invited. We need to study for Science."

She sits up. Lights a cigarette. There could be nothing but spicy mustard in the fridge, but Mom always has cigarettes.

"You're studying a lot these days."

"Trying my best," I say.

"Good girl." She taps her bed, inviting me to sit. Like she used to. I used to love sitting with her here. She'd braid my hair and ask me about school. She'd joke around that I was nothing but trouble, then we'd stay up watching old movies and eating marshmallows. When she used to be fun.

I sit on the bed. The comforter feels dusty. Grimy. Stuffy. I don't think Mom has done laundry in a while.

"School ok?" she asks, pushing my grown-out bangs behind my ear. "You doing all right?"

Now. Show it to her now. "School is fine. There's this thing . . ." I start to say, but she's coughing again. It's a deep, rolling cough like the sea is stuck in her lungs. She holds up a hand for me to wait. Balances her cigarette in the astray. Catches her breath.

"What is it?" she asks.

I hand her the permission form. She clears her throat a million times while she tries to focus. I can tell by her glassy eyes she's taken her medication recently, and maybe more than she should. Her eyes have a hard time following the words on the page. I give her time.

"College?" she asks.

"Visits. To learn about the programs."

"You want to go to these schools?"

"Maybe."

"How are you going to pull that off?" All her tenderness is gone. Everything that makes her Mom dissolves and curls away with the smoke from her cigarette.

"I mean, I'm doing okay at school. I'm passing History this year, and I'll graduate."

"Yeah. And then what? It's not all about smarts. How will you get there?"

"Most kids get an apartment in the city." She *pffts* and leans back on her headboard, then takes a drag on her cigarette. "Lily and I can be roommates. Get jobs. I could do my courses part-time so I can work too."

"You've got it all figured out?"

"No. Which is why I want to go to the open house."

"Twenty dollars?" She looks up at me. "You've got to be kidding me."

"Lily will lend me the money." White lie.

"A loan means you have to pay it back."

"I offered to take her shifts in the Leadership project." Bigger lie. She knows Lily but doesn't remember how generous she is. If Lily knew I needed money, she'd never loan it to me. She'd give it up without asking to be repaid. Mom still doesn't sign it. "What is it?" I ask.

"You want to leave home?"

Hell. Yeah.

"I want to go to school."

"You'll have to move out."

And never look back.

"Yeah."

"You'll have to leave me." She taps her cigarette into the ashtray. I feel like a pile of stale ash in a heap waiting to be blown away.

"I could take the bus home on weekends. Summer."

But I won't. And she knows it.

"I'll have to live in the city," I say.

"If you move out, completely, I can't get money anymore to support you." She must be kidding. What support? I spent my last six bucks, money my aunt in Montreal sent me for Christmas, on sliced cheese and eggs. I stole money. But the thought of leaving Mom fills me with the urge to pack and run, but also . . . also, I don't want to leave her. Because she's the person who taught me how to bake apple pie, and how to say no to boys without being a bitch, and who made me laugh until I peed myself. She's mine. And I'm hers.

Or at least, we used to be each other's.

"What about sticking around here? Get a job, like you said, and help me out. A year. Maybe two. Save up for college?"

Her words are anchors. Hands pulling me, pushing me down into the water. No scuba mask.

"I want to go now. Like everyone else. Please, sign the paper." Her eyes flutter. Her head bobs to the front. She's drifting. Fading. She might disappear in her bed for another few hours. "I'm not packing my bags or anything. It's a visit. To learn more." She hands me the paper. Not signed. She crushes her cigarette in the ashtray and rolls over.

I've never cheated or lied much about anything serious. But in one day, I stole money from school and forged my mother's signature. Some lies are secrets. And some secrets have to be kept hidden.

Chapter 5
Dinner Party

"Finally," Lily says, opening her front door. Beast, her overexcited German Shepherd, practically knocks me down, licking my face as I untie my shoes. I'm out of breath from the uphill bike ride in the slush. Tamara is yelling something from inside the house. "The Tempest is in full hurricane mode. You've been warned," Lily says, pulling Beast away by his collar.

The house smells warm and salty. I smell bay leaves and rosemary, meat and potatoes. My stomach growls.

Tamara comes running to the door. "Élise! It's my birthday! We're having cake!" And she's already off again.

"We're studying in the bedroom room, so off-limits," Lily cries out to Tamara.

I place my shoes next to Lily's in the entrance and walk in. "Hi, Élise, hope you're hungry," Lily's mom says.

Me? Hungry? Only always.

"Smells great, Mrs. McLeod," I say, waving at her.

"Beef stew and ravioli. Tamara couldn't decide, so we'll have both." Lily rolls her eyes.

"Thanks for inviting me."

"Ten minutes 'til supper," Lily's mom tells us.

I follow Lily to her room and set my bag next to the desk between the two beds. Lily's side is decorated with black and white photos of Elvis, James Dean, and The Beatles. It's like her side of the room is in a time warp. Tamara has pictures of pop singers and a Montreal Canadiens flag above her bed. They couldn't be more different.

"Did you get it signed?" she asks.

"Yes. You're obsessed."

"I prefer the word *passionate*."

"Passionately obsessed."

"It's going to be great. I've been looking up the schools and programs online."

Of course she has.

"I like Marianopolis. It's a smaller school. More intimate, you know. We can get to know our teachers better." I make a face like I'm ready to puke. "It's not like high school. In college, teachers have meaningful conversations with their students. It's not all about following rules." Lily unpacks her science books. "Anyway, it looks great. But it's private. And expensive."

"What about the other schools?"

"Dawson has about a million programs." She turns on her tablet to show me their course list. "I'm thinking commerce. Or creative arts, or something, I don't know yet.

But for you . . ." She hands me the tablet. I read the heading: *ALC: Arts, Literature, and Communications.* "It includes visual arts, design, media, literature. I think you'd be amazing. They have the same program at Marianopolis."

"Private school? No way," I say.

"We can get jobs."

"I'll have to get one anyway. And we'll need a place to stay. And books. It'll get expensive."

"We'll figure it out. And our parents will help." My insides twist. And knot. It's like I'm cut in half through the stomach.

Lily looks down as she says it. She realizes her mistake. Money has always been tight with Mom. I shop at thrift stores and Lily doesn't. I accept reused school supplies from the student services office, and Lily always has brand-new pencil cases and binders each year. I think these things are obvious to her, but I guess when you don't really need to worry about money, you forget others do, and right now Lily is so hyper-focused on college, she didn't think.

"Supper!" Lily's mom calls. Tamara comes running out of somewhere, her feet pounding the wooden floors, shaking the whole house. I force a smile and take a seat at the table.

We all toast a happy birthday to Tamara with sparkling apple juice. She's beaming. We dig in, and it's probably the most delicious thing I've had in ages. Everyone has two bowls: one for the stew and another for the ravioli, but my bowls are extra full. I could never eat this in one sitting, but I don't want to be rude. I eat some of each dish but leave about half.

"Too much?" Lily's mom asks.

"It's delicious," I say.

"No problem. You can take it home. I'll pack it up for you."

"Thanks."

There's cake and ice cream afterward. I give Tamara a card I drew for her of a fairy fighting a dragon. "It's amazing. I love it," Tamara says.

Lily's mom reaches over to take the card from Tamara. "My goodness, Élise, so talented. We can frame it," she suggests.

"Cool," Tamara agrees and goes on to open a gift from Lily and her mom. "Yes!" she says, discovering a new pink kick scooter. "Thanks! Can I take it out now?"

"In the snow?" her mom asks.

"It's almost all melted."

Mrs. McLeod considers it. "Helmet," she says.

"Yes!"

Lily and I help her mom clear the table, then we get to studying. Science is not my best subject, but Lily breaks it down for me and we review her notes. After an hour and a half, I'm beat.

"I should go," I say.

Lily leads me to the door, and I want to remind her about the leftovers her mom offered, but it's too awkward. Taking them means I'd have a decent lunch for a few days. I can make it last all week if I need to. I linger in the doorway, tying my shoes real slow, hoping Lily will remember, but I don't say anything about it.

"Don't forget to see the guidance counsellor tomorrow

with your permission form. I'm turning mine in first thing in the morning to be sure to get a spot on the trip."

"Noted. See you tomorrow."

Tamara comes rolling down the driveway with her scooter, wearing a smile so happy and wild it almost makes me want a new scooter too.

"Bye, Élise!" she says, pushing the scooter in a circle around me. She hops off to give me a hug, and it's so strong even though she is so small. It's almost like being attacked by Beast. "Thanks for the card, I love it."

"You're welcome," I say, then tie the clasp on my helmet and hop on my bike. "See ya!"

"Wait!" Lily's mom comes running through the house with a plastic bag. "You almost forgot." She's got my leftovers in her hand. She moves past Lily in the door frame. "Lily, could you please feed Beast before he starts chewing up my shoes again?"

"Bye!" Lily calls out and disappears into the house.

Lily's mom holds the bag out to me. I could kiss her. "Thank you. So much," I say. I want to say more. I want to thank her for purposely filling my bowls to maximum capacity, but I can't.

"There's enough for a few days. And for your mom too." I look at the ground. Take the bag. Adjust my handlebars. "How is she?" Mrs. McLeod asks.

I have to choose my words carefully. If I'm too 'fine,' she'll know it's not true. If I tell the truth, she'll worry. "She's getting better," I say.

"That's great to hear. It would be nice to have one of our famous brunches. All together."

"I'd like that." At least that isn't a lie.

"I can call her. Set up a date?"

Crap. Wrong answer. "I don't know if she'll come. She's been feeling pretty reclusive lately."

"Yeah?"

Now I have to talk. I have to say more. "She's better but still in lots of pain. I don't think she likes people seeing her look weak, or whatever."

"That's silly. We're friends. You're practically family." She bites her lip. If I'm family, I'm like a daughter. But I have a mom. Sort of.

"Thanks, Mrs. McLeod. For supper. For leftovers." I hold up the bag.

Don't cry. Don't cry. Don't cry. "This helps a lot," I say and ride off toward home, the wind in my face making my eyes water.

It's dark when I bike home, but my neighbour Ginette's porch light is on, and there's a blue car parked in the driveway we share with her. She sees me ride up. She waves from her usual spot, smoking her cigarette and petting Ferry. He pulls free from her, jumps from the railing on her porch, and wraps his tail around my leg until I pet him. He rolls over and I feel his whole belly purring softly.

I found Ferry when he was a kitten. He was skinny and his fur was patchy. I fed him and took care of him. When he started scratching up the furniture, Mom said he was rehabilitated enough to be an authentic alley cat. He does okay on his own, but Ginette and I still treat him once in a while, so he comes by for visits often enough. Sometimes when he scratches at the screen door I sneak him into my room for the night. He'll sit on my lap and purr. It's probably because I give him leftovers, but it still feels warm, sweet, and friendly. We never knew what to call him until Ginette named him Ferry because he goes back and forth between her house and ours.

I wave back to Ginette and peek into the window of the compact car. A Toyota. Rusted. Old. There are fast-food wrappers and empty cups littered all over the car. Cigarette butts fill the cup holder. A cooler sits in the back seat along with four brown paper bags rolled up at the top. I have no idea whose car it is.

"Visitor?" Ginette calls out.

"I guess," I say. No one ever visits. Since Mom's accident, only Aunt Terry has come by. Once.

I open the door. "Mom?" Nothing. "Mom, I'm home."

There's a bass beat coming from Mom's room. The house stinks. A dull, skunky smell. Apparently, my mom smokes pot now. "Mom!" I yell it now.

"Élise?"

Who else?

A minute later the music stops. Mom opens her door an inch and pokes her head out. A cloud of smoke surrounds her. Through the gap in the door, I can see a man lying on her bed. "You're home early," she says.

"It's almost nine. I have school tomorrow."

"I thought you might be sleeping over at your friend's house."

"Who's that?" I ask, pointing, totally grossed out about the random person in her room. The man stands up from the bed in a T-shirt and boxer shorts. He moves to the door and stands behind Mom. Close behind her. He's about to speak, but Mom turns to him, puts a hand to his chest, and he turns away. The fog of smoke envelops him, and he disappears back into Mom's room.

"He's leaving. Go to bed," Mom says. She almost sounds like she used to. Soft voice, almost sweet, like when I was a kid.

I head straight to my room, then remember the leftovers. I walk back out to refrigerate them. The croissants and cheese are gone. The egg carton holds two eggs. Looks like Mom had a dinner party. Perfect. There's a paper bag on the counter, like the ones I saw in the back seat of the car. Mom's door is completely closed. I peek in the bag. Two full pill bottles. Big white pills, like the ones Mom takes for her pain. But there is no prescription label on these. There's laughter coming from her room. It's not Mom; it's him. I step closer to her door, but it's quiet now. And then it isn't. I slam my bedroom door behind me. I rush to put on my headphones to keep the noise out.

Punk rock. Grunge. Opera. Anything loud enough to drown out the sounds from Mom's room.

Chapter 6
Stranger Danger

I am the champion of awkward situations. If only I knew how to navigate them. High school doesn't prepare you for waking up to a stranger in your house. Mr. Stranger Danger is in the living room, his feet up on the couch. Eating my beef stew.

"That's mine," I say. I understand animals. The whole protecting your territory thing. Food. It's all about food.

Stranger Danger turns around. His long hair is tied in a ponytail. He has wrinkly skin around his eyes and a bushy beard. He stands with a fork in one hand, beef stew container in the other. Lipstick-smacked boxers. "The food. It's mine," I repeat.

"Sorry, kid. It was the only thing in here."

"There's a corner store down the hill. They have food."

He puts the container down on the coffee table. I'm ready to pounce.

Mom's bedroom door creaks open. Her hair is a tangled net with who-knows-what living in it. She's in shorts and a Jack Daniel's sweatshirt. She smells like stale weed and sweat.

"You said you were on your way out," Mom says to Stranger Danger.

"This is good stuff. You cook?"

"No," Mom says. "We gotta get ready for our day, so you can head out." She pulls on the drawstrings of her hoodie.

Stranger Danger lights a joint. It's seven in the morning. Smoke wafts in front of him and lingers there. It stinks so bad I think I might be sick. I can't help coughing. I walk past him to the door to get some air, but he grabs my wrist as I walk by.

"Hey," I say. "Let go."

"Relax, girl," he says. Mom's eyes are wide. Not re-laxed. Bells ringing, flags raised. This guy is a bad seed.

"Hey. Leave her alone," Mom says, her voice gruff.

"Calm down, would you? Not into little girls." No way am I going to correct him. "If you're headed out, grab one of the paper bags in my back seat." He looks at Mom. "A small one." He releases my arm.

"Get it yourself," I say to Mom.

"Oh, man, you've got your hands full with this one, Claire."

"Are you done with my lunch?" I ask.

"Sorry. Didn't know it was yours." Because me living here didn't give it away. I step out onto the porch.

Ginette is on her balcony again. Smoking. Like always. She waves at me. "Everything okay over there?" she asks.

Where do I start? "Yeah. Thanks, Ginette." She waves again.

Mom comes out and opens Stranger Danger's car.

"Where is he?" I ask.

"Bathroom. He's leaving."

"What the hell, Mom?"

Her head is in the back seat. She's bent over, her butt in the air, and I want to give her a hard kick. "He's a friend," she says. Her voice is shaking like a leaf hanging onto a tree in a fall storm. A paper bag crinkles. She steps out of the car, looking into the bag.

"Friend?" I say. "I'm not stupid. And there's a bag of pills on the counter. What's that?"

"Friends bring gifts," she says.

"Gifts?"

She pulls out four fifty-dollar bills from the bag and puts them in her pocket. She takes them out again and hands me one. I swear it's dripping in grime and puke and shit for how dirty it feels to be holding this money. "Get groceries after school," she says. She puts the rest back in her pocket.

"He brings you pills. And money. Because you . . ." I can't say it. She looks like she's freezing in her shorts. She's stepping from side to side like a toddler who has to pee. "Mom?"

"I didn't think you'd be home," she says.

I want to punish her. Ground her. Yell. But she looks drained, a pale-green exhausted version of my mom who used to let me win at Scrabble and showed me how to ride my bike. "Mom?"

Stranger Danger slaps the screen door open. Mom takes a step back. "Do I need to check, Claire?"

"Only took what's mine," she says, shaky-leaf voice so frail and tired. She takes another step back.

"Good." He tries to slap her on the butt, but she turns and he misses. "We'll keep it in the bedroom, then?" I'm going to puke. He gets into his car and drives off. Mom is already inside. She closes her bedroom door. The pill bottle shakes. The bed creaks.

I have to get ready for school.

Chapter 7
Hope, for Now

It's finally lunchtime. At least Stranger Danger left me enough stew for my lunch. I eat in the art room as I finish up my project before meeting Lily in the cafeteria.

"Finally. Let's get our permission forms to the guidance counsellor. Spots are filling up quick." She holds my hand and pulls me up the stairs toward the office. We cross our Leadership teacher in the stairway, looking rushed and annoyed, as always, but he stops.

"Élise. I've been looking for you." Shit. "You collected quite a bit of money yesterday during your sales."

"I guess lots of people needed the sugar rush," I say.

"Yes, well, there was a miscalculation with the spreadsheet and the amount of money in the cashbox."

"Oh."

"Oh, yeah," Lily says. "The donations, remember?"

"Well, yes, that's where things are unclear." He pulls the spreadsheet out of his pocket and unfolds it to show me. Lily stands next to him and points at the column she created.

"See, it's all here," Lily says.

"There should have been fourteen extra dollars in the cashbox. But instead, we're six dollars short."

"Not possible." Lily grabs the spreadsheet. "I'll count it again, sir, I'm sure there's some mistake," she says. "I'll bring it back in a few minutes. We're headed to the guidance counsellor to hand in our permission forms. We're in a bit of a hurry, but I promise to settle this right after."

Our teacher looks at Lily, then at me. "All right. Thanks. Then please bring it back so today's students can take their turn selling cookies."

"You bet," Lily says.

We continue up the steps. "Did you miss something yesterday?" she asks me.

"I don't think so, but it was kind of crazy at the end of lunch with the soccer team buying everything. I might have forgotten something."

We reach the guidance counsellor's office, and Lily knocks. Mr. Hanes opens his door. His thick black glasses make his eyes look huge. He's kind of old-looking, but he wears cargo pants and sneakers all the time. I imagine him spending weekends in front of a fancy gaming console. "Hi, girls. Here about the field trip?" His smile is friendly and kind. He opens his door wider to let us in. Lily hands him an envelope. He opens it and sets her permission slip and money aside.

I hand him a wrinkled twenty-dollar bill and my folded

permission slip. He looks at the signature. Then at me. "I'm glad you're both coming. After the trip next Thursday, I can make an appointment with each of you to discuss your interests and fill out your college applications, if you're ready."

"Can I make my appointment now?" Lily asks.

"Sure," Mr. Hanes says. Lily sets her appointment for next Friday afternoon. They both look at me.

"Um. Yeah. Me too."

"Okay. I'll put you down after Lily. I like to meet each student individually." This is a relief. I love Lily, but when it comes to talking about school and college, she gets crazy obsessive and hyper-focused, and it's hard to get a word in.

"What's with the cashbox?" Mr. Hanes asks.

Lily explains the mix-up. I try not to look worried or guilty, but then Lily asks if we can use his office to recount the money. He nods, and Lily sets up at a desk in the back of his office and starts counting. She reads over the spreadsheet.

"He's right. Six dollars short and no donation. Twenty dollars is missing? How did you miscount twenty dollars?" She starts counting the money again.

I feel like an idiot. My best friend has all the trust in the world for me, and I did something so dumb without even thinking about it. Of course I'd get caught. But I'd rather get caught with Lily and Mr. Hanes than our super-strict Leadership teacher. I want to cry. Like when I was ten and lied about taking Mom's lipstick.

I stare at my mismatched socks. They never match.

"Élise?" Mr. Hanes says. "Your History teacher says you're picking up your marks. Do you have time to chat now?" I look over at Lily who's still counting money.

"Sure."

"Great. Lily, do you mind if Élise meets up with you in a few minutes?"

"Oh. Yeah. Sure. I'll be in the library. I'll figure this out," she says to me, tapping the cashbox.

"Leave it," I say. "I was on duty yesterday. I'll count it again. I'll figure it out."

"But they need it downstairs," Lily says.

"I'll be quick," I say. She gives me a pained look like maybe she doesn't trust me to count it, but she hands me the cashbox and leaves. Mr. Hanes closes his office door behind her.

"Is this your mom's signature?" Mr. Hanes asks, holding up my permission form.

"No," I say. I can tell there's no point in lying to him. He leans back in his chair. "I forged it."

"Why?" he asks.

"Because she doesn't want me to go."

"Why not?"

Deep breath.

"Mom doesn't want me to leave town for college."

"Does she have a reason?"

"She's still not herself. Not since her accident last year."

"I didn't realize her injuries were so bad," Mr. Hanes says.

"She almost drove off the overpass. Messed up her back. She still needs help and doesn't want to be alone."

"I hear you." He crosses his arms. "But what about you? What do you want?"

"College sounds cool. Expensive, though. Not sure how I'd even manage."

"Your pre-university college program will only cost a few hundred bucks in fees and books. University, McGill or Concordia, will cost more, but we're lucky in Quebec. Tuition is low compared to other provinces. You can apply for a loan. Or a scholarship. Student housing is available for manageable rent prices. We can find you a job near school. Lots of kids with the same challenges get by."

I play with the handle on the cashbox. "You can help me with all that?" I ask.

"Of course. Whatever you need. I'm here to help you stay in school. Whatever it takes."

"Okay."

"What about your mom is holding you back?"

"Everything," I say. "She can't drive. She has a hard time walking, shovelling, cleaning. Regular stuff." I don't mention how she's locked up in her room all day, with strange men and painkillers.

"House stuff?" he says. I nod. "There are services available to help her with those things if she's physically unable to do them for herself."

I bite the inside of my cheek and think about it. "I don't think Mom would accept help."

"There's more to it?"

"Yeah."

"Tell me about it," he says and motions for me to sit in the armchair across from him.

I tell him. Not everything. But I tell him about having almost no food in the fridge until Mom gets her disability money. I tell him how Mom sleeps a lot because of the pain medication. "I'm working my butt off to graduate. But it might be for nothing," I say. I think he'll be surprised. I think I'll feel like a pitiful piece of crap telling him these things, but I don't.

"Tell you what. I'll talk to your mom about the field trip."

"What?"

"Legally, she needs to know you're leaving school property. But I'll explain it's part of school and you're attending to get information."

"She won't agree to it."

"You'd be surprised how convincing I can be. And I'll waive the fee." He opens my crinkled twenty-dollar bill and hands it to me. "Keep it. I don't think anyone should have to pay for this trip, but budget cuts, blah blah blah. There are enough students going to cover the cost of renting the bus. Nothing you need to worry about."

"Thanks."

"Promise me you'll come, and keep your appointment afterward."

"I promise."

"All right. You have somewhere to be. Go meet Lily before she blows up trying to figure out the cashbox mystery."

I don't know what to say. He's summed me up so well, knows I took the money, and is not reacting the way an adult should.

"Thank you, Mr. Hancs. I don't think I could figure this stuff out on my own."

"It's why I'm paid the big bucks," he says, smiling.

I drag my feet to the cafeteria and hand my classmates at the bake-sale table the cashbox. They flip their closed sign to open. Lily meets me at the table. "So?"

"Money is all there."

"Really?"

"Yeah."

"I miscounted?"

"I guess." I feel terrible making her feel like she did something wrong, but one admission of guilt today is all I can handle.

"Okay." A comfortable best-friend-only silence moves between us, but it's heavier than usual. The silence is carrying Lily's suspicions, but she lets it go.

For now.

Chapter 8
Nobody's Business

When I step off the school bus and walk home, Ginette is on her porch, smoking. She's like a statue, always in the same position. One arm over the railing, waving, the other holding a cigarette to her mouth. Except today she's not petting Ferry the cat. I wave back.

"Ferry out hunting?" I ask.

She shrugs. "Haven't seen him since this morning. I'll put out some tuna tonight. He'll be back." Sometimes he's gone for a few days, but he always shows up when we feed him. I'm about to pull out my key to unlock the door, but Mom opens it. The circles under her eyes are dark and deep. She smells like smoke.

"What did you do?" she asks.

"Hi, Mom." I push past her and into the house. She follows me, and the screen door bangs on the doorframe.

"You signed the paper," she says.

"I want to go."

"Now your teacher knows we don't have enough cash for you to go."

"Guidance counsellor."

"Whatever. He was asking a whole bunch of questions."

"Like what?"

"How I'm doing since the accident, if we're eating okay, if you have everything you need. I don't like people getting in my business."

"He cares about what happens to me after graduation. It's his job." I turn my back to her, but she pulls my arm and swings it so hard, I spin around. I knock the fake flowers hanging from a hook above her doorframe, and the pot swings. Dust from the plastic leaves flies through the air. Mom's hand is on my throat as she pushes me to the wall. She squeezes.

"You don't say anything about anything. Keep quiet." I turn my head like I saw someone in a self-defence video do, and I get some air. She holds me tighter.

"You can't go around telling your school about anything," Stranger Danger says, walking out of Mom's room. He's tucking a chequered shirt into his pants. Tightening his belt.

"Rich, I've got this," Mom says, loosening her grip around my throat. It's enough for me to turn, duck under her arm, and get away from her. She stumbles and holds the wall for balance.

I rub my neck. "What the hell?" I say. "I didn't say anything. I told him I want to go on a field trip. That's it."

"You make sure that's all it is," Rich says.

"Or what?" I ask, still rubbing my throat. I know it's a mistake the second I've said it. Rich grabs my wrist. Twists my arm behind my back. Grabs my other arm and holds both my wrists in his giant hand. He smells of smoke, booze, wet mop, and old meat. He's stronger than Mom. I try to wriggle free.

"Or nothing," he whispers in my ear. "Except I know where to make bruises no one will ever see." His breath is hot and stale.

A scratching at the screen door has us both turning. Ferry growls. And hisses.

"This thing yours?" Rich asks Mom, his hand still tight around my wrists.

"Stray," she says. Ferry continues scratching to get inside.

Outside, we hear Ginette whistling for Ferry. Rich cocks his head to one side.

"Neighbour," Mom says. "A nosy one, but she never comes over."

Ferry is going to tear up the screen door. Not that it matters.

"Dumb cat," Rich says, letting go of me to kick at the door and ward Ferry away. "Don't," I say. "He just wants to say hi." I open the door and pick up Ferry. He nestles into the crook of my neck. He's warm.

"Probably full of diseases. And fleas," Mom says.

I want to say, *Not much different from you two*, but I hold off. I head to my room with Ferry in my arms, and Mom turns on me again. "You keep quiet about our business," she repeats. "Or you'll end up like Ferry: homeless and alone."

I purse my lips.

Zip them.

Throw away the key.

Mom marches into her room. Rich follows. But it's like Mom's still got me pinned to the wall. Still trapped. And shaking.

Ferry lies on my stomach and purrs softly. I think I'll let him stay the night.

Chapter 9
Dawson College

I've spent most of the last week in my room or at Lily's house studying for our next science test. But today I can relax. We're on the bus, ready to leave for the city, and the air is popping with excitement. Lily and I have never been to the city together. The last time I was in Montreal was after Mom's accident, when I stayed with Aunt Terry. Mom and Terry argue over everything, so I haven't been back since.

There's traffic on the highway and while some students are getting restless, I'm enjoying the view of the city coming into focus. Traffic, busy streets, and the Olympic Stadium ahead. It's like another world from the vast corn fields and silos of home. Joliette is only an hour from civilization, but I might as well be living on Mars.

The bus drops us off at the Viau metro station; we're meant to take the subway downtown. "The metro is part of the experience," Mr. Hanes says as he ushers us off the bus. We buy our metro tickets and then walk down some stairs, an escalator, and more stairs — down what feels like thousands of feet — until we reach a platform. The air is musty and still. The smell is a mixture of moldy, wet something, and urine. We're told to get off at the Atwater stop where we can walk through the underground tunnels directly into Dawson College.

We step off the metro car and walk up another million steps from the platform. We're in the basement of the school, which is an open area lined with lockers and stairs. We climb up to street level and are met with a wide, open atrium. Stations are set up around the space, each labelled with a different program, hundreds of students circulating.

Lily is next to me and squeezes my hand. "This. Is. Awesome," she says.

Students zip past, in and out of the atrium. Some sit at tables, eating or playing cards.

"Welcome, everyone!" A student a few years older greets us. She's wearing a blue vest with *Dawson College* embroidered on the front over a crop top. Her nametag reads *J.T.* Her pink hair is in a buzz cut with a fade on the sides. She wears baggy jeans with holes in the knees. We aren't allowed to dress like that at school.

J.T. gives us a tour of the building. I expected it to be quiet while classes are in session, but the atrium is a noisy, bustling place. My favourite place J.T. shows us is the library. It's in a gigantic domed hall with stained-glass windows. It used to be a chapel. It's big and bright. Reading and studying are not my favourite thing, but I can picture myself drawing and creating in this space. Dawson is so different from our two-storey high school where we have to ask permission to blow our noses.

We return to the atrium to visit with students from different programs. Lily is beaming. She takes pamphlets from every station. I look around to figure out where to go when J.T. approaches me.

"See anything you like?" J.T. holds a clipboard to her chest.

"Not sure."

"Can I show you around?"

"Yeah. Thanks."

We walk through the centre of the exhibits. "You more into science and STEM or humanities and literature?" Gibberish.

"I like to draw," I say. I sound like a three-year-old.

"Visual arts? Media?"

"Yeah," I say.

"The ALC program — Arts, Literature, and Communication — might be right for you. It's a mix of creative arts. Lots of computer stuff too."

"Is that what you're studying?" I ask.

"I'm in pure and applied sciences."

I tighten the straps of my backpack. "Sounds hard."

"It's a challenge. I love it, though. I think I might go into engineering once I get to university. But let's focus on you. Jen and Mark can answer your questions about ALC."

I search for Lily's red hair, but I don't see her anywhere. I don't even know what to ask these students, but they ask me first. They ask about what creative arts I like, and when I tell them I like to draw, they ask to see my sketchbook.

"How do you know I have it with me?" I ask.

"An artist always has one. Like a writer always has a notebook," Jen says.

"I have both," I admit.

"Let's see it," Mark says. I never show anyone my drawings. But I don't know these people. Somehow, it's less embarrassing to show them than to show Lily. I open my book to a drawing of Ferry.

"Wow," J.T. says, looking over my shoulder.

"Cute," Jen says. *Cute.* Not good, *cute.* I flip the page. "Oh. This one . . ." she says, placing her hand on the page to keep me from turning it. "This one is . . . wow." I turn it around to look at it right-side-up. It's a sketch of Mom on the couch. She has one knee up, her hand limp with a cigarette between two fingers. Her hair is in a messy bun. Her laugh lines and dimples are shaded in. She was laughing at something stupid on TV. She was about to turn to me, so we see a little more than her profile. She's relaxed. Almost happy, but like something is brewing beneath it all. I drew this about two months ago. On a good day.

"See, I could never do that," J.T. says. "You're really good."

"Thanks." I feel my cheeks warm. "It's my mom."

"It's so real," Jen says. "Do you always use pencil and paper for your drawings?"

"Mostly. Sometimes charcoal. Or Pastels."

"How about digital stuff?" Mark asks. I shake my head. He stands next to me with his iPad and shows me some graphic drawings he's working on. One is of a minotaur, and he shows me how he's animated the drawings.

"So cool," I say.

"In ALC, you learn how to use different traditional and graphic media to create illustrations, animation, video games. There are poetry and lit classes, too, even journalism. It's broad."

I look at the expensive tablet in his hand.

"Great job, Mark," J.T. says.

"Your drawings are amazing," I say.

"Thanks," he says, setting the tablet down.

"Do you have to buy a lot of your own material and books?"

"Some supplies are provided, but yeah, you'll need to get equipped." I think he notices me deflate. "We have a bookstore here with all the books you'll need for the program. You can buy most of them second-hand. Supplies too. Even electronics."

"Good to know," I say.

"You can also apply for loans and bursaries. There are ways to help your parents pay for your stuff."

"Right," I say.

Mark is being helpful, but when he mentions my parents, I feel like a little kid, lost in this huge space. "Thanks a lot," I say, clutching my sketchbook.

I walk back to the centre of the atrium with J.T. "There are lots of jobs available on campus. In the cafeteria, the library, the bookstore. If you're looking. I work in the student services centre. We get listings from local businesses, too, looking for employees. Being downtown has its perks. There are job opportunities close to school everywhere."

"How about apartments?"

"Right. You all live outside the city."

"Yeah."

"There is student housing available for your first year. After that, you need to find an apartment. Moving sucks, though. Apartments off campus are more expensive, but once you get to know a few people, you can find a roommate."

"You from Montreal?" I ask.

"Yeah. Westmount." I don't know much about Montreal neighbourhoods, but I know Westmount is an old, rich part of the city. I'd imagine ladies in pencil skirts and suits going to high-paying jobs. I wouldn't picture J.T. "I take the bus. On nice days I walk."

"Cool," I say.

"Maybe this can help." She digs into her pocket and opens a Marvel-stamped Velcro wallet. She pulls out a business card. "The student services offices can help you find a place. People tend to move out of smaller apartments often, so the rent is more reasonable. If you have someone to share the cost, we can help find you something."

"Really?"

"Yeah. My number is on the back. If you have more questions, you can text me anytime."

"Thank you."

"No problem." I take the card from her and balance my sketchpad on one knee to reach my wallet. "Let me," J.T. says, taking it from me. "This really is beautiful."

"Thanks."

"I should get everyone gathered up. I think your school is leaving soon. Hope to see you around next year," she says.

"Me too."

We approach the others, and I find Lily talking to Mr. Hanes, showing him all the pamphlets she's collected. J.T. instructs us to start heading out so we can make room for the next batch of high school visitors. She thanks us and encourages us to fill out our applications in the next few days, as programs will be filling up fast. We all thank her, and Mr. Hanes guides us back to the basement and to the metro.

On the bus back to Joliette, I think Dawson might be a good fit, but I don't know how I can possibly make enough money to pay for everything. The next problem is convincing Mom to let me leave.

Chapter 10
Cat Got Your Tongue?

I wake up at 6:00 a.m. to Stranger Danger crunching toast in my kitchen. I hadn't figured him for an early riser. I turn to head back to my room, but he stops me.

"Hey," he says. "I think we got off to a faulty start the other day." No way is he trying to be human.

"Yeah," I say.

"I'm Rich. Richard."

"Hi."

"You're Élise. Nice to meet you. Look, your mom and I . . ." I fight the urgent need to place my hands over my ears and run screaming from the room. My insides are like twisted barbed wire. "I'll be around more often." *Ew.* "And the other day, the . . . deliveries, in my car."

"I don't need to know."

"Then we agree. And you don't need to mention a

thing about me being here. Not to anyone."

"You made it clear enough," I say, rubbing my wrists. He was right. It hurt when he was holding them, but he left no bruises.

"Let me make it clearer." For a big hairy guy, he moves quickly. He's towering over me. He blows smoke in my face and I gag. "You won't say a word about me." His hands squeeze my cheeks so my lips pucker. I fight back and try to push him away. I push right into his chest, but he smiles and tucks his long hair behind his ear. I stop struggling as he lightens his grasp. "Cat got your tongue? Good. The way I like it." He goes back to the table to finish his breakfast. "Your mom gave you money for food?" he asks.

I rub my cheek. "Yeah."

"Then buy food. This place is a fucking disaster."

I throw on clean clothes, don't bother with a shower, and leave for the bus stop earlier than I need to. *Le Dépanneur* is the only thing open at this time, so I get myself a muffin and a hot chocolate for breakfast, trying hard not to spill it. I realize I have no appetite. I burn my tongue on the too-hot chocolate and chuck it in the garbage. I take a bite of the muffin, but I can't get the taste of Rich's breath out of my mouth. I throw that away too. Money wasted. I feel hopeless, standing outside for the school bus. The sun is barely making its way above the hills facing me. My legs start to go numb from cold by the time it's daylight. Then the rest of me goes cold when a blue car pulls up to me. Stranger Danger. Rich. The window comes down.

"Need a lift?" he asks.

Not even if you paid me, Rich.

The bus appears at the crest of the hill, thank god. "Bus is here."

He looks in his rear-view mirror. "You forgot this at home." He leans over to the passenger window. He hands me my agenda, open to today. In my handwriting, I read *guidance appointment, noon.* It's a reminder for my appointment with Mr. Hanes.

I take my agenda from him. Rich's fingernails are grimy. One is black, like the nail might fall off any minute.

"Aren't you going to say thanks?" he asks.

"The appointment is about college applications."

"Guidance counsellors ask questions." The bus is taking forever to come down the hill. "You sure you don't want a lift to school?" I clutch my agenda to my chest. "Maybe some other time, then. Remember what we talked about."

The bus brakes and squeals to a stop. The driver opens the doors.

"And, Élise?" Rich looks out the passenger window. "Don't say a thing to your pretty red-headed friend, either," he says, before speeding off.

My legs prickle as I climb the bus steps, like when your leg falls asleep and you want to move it, but it feels too weird. Lily is sitting at the back of the bus, peering out her window.

"Were you talking to someone outside?"

"Someone asking for directions," I lie.

"Ready for your meeting with Mr. Hanes?" I can barely hear her over my heart exploding in my chest.

"Sure," I say.

But I skip the appointment and avoid Lily at lunch. I head to the art room, but Mr. Hanes finds me there.

"So this is where you're hiding." Mr. Hanes's voice is loud enough to pierce through my headphones. I scramble to turn my music down. "Did you forget about our appointment?"

"I'm so sorry." I pull my science notes out from under my binder. "I needed to cram for my science test," I say, my hands smudged with ink. My completed drawing is drying in front of me. "I mean, since I'm done with this," I add, sliding my artwork across the table.

"May I?" Mr. Hanes says, turning my drawing around so he can see it.

"Sure."

"It's okay that you were working on this instead of meeting with me. Or studying. It's beautiful," Mr. Hanes says. "It's so bright."

"It's supposed to be dark." He tilts his head to look at it harder. "The assignment was a pen and ink drawing of the night sky," I say.

"Well, the sky is dark, but the moon is casting light all over it. It's stunning."

"Thanks," I say, looking at it again myself. I still see darkness.

"We can meet Monday, then. I'm curious to hear what you thought about the visit."

"I'll be there," I say, only half believing myself.

"There you are," Lily says, walking into the art room, out of breath. "Oh, hey, Mr. Hanes. Tell me she came to her appointment."

"We were rescheduling," Mr. Hanes says. Lily gives me

a look like a mother scolding a three-year-old. She looks a lot like her mom in this moment. "I'll see you Monday, then?" Mr. Hanes says, on his way out.

"She'll be there," Lily says. When he's gone, Lily turns to me, and the disappointment on her face makes her cheeks as red as her hair. "I thought you'd fill out an application."

"I will."

"What are you doing here, anyway?" she asks.

I show her my science notes, but she sees my drawing.

"We can study tonight."

"It's Friday."

"We'll kick your procrastination habit."

"Fine." Lily is shifting her weight from one foot to the other, like she has to pee, or like she can't contain her excitement. "What?" I ask.

"I filled out my application."

"Great! What for?

"Social Sciences at Dawson as first choice, you know, to give me the whole general knowledge thing, and we'd be right downtown. Lots of history and lit classes." Her excitement is contagious.

"I'll go see him Monday. I'll do it."

"Please don't make me go to college without you," she says.

"I'll try, Lily." And I mean it. I want to give it a shot. It's like her to push and pull out all the arguments why I can do it, and she'd likely convince me to fill out my application with her right now, but she can tell something is up. And I love her for not asking.

"You'll come by after supper?" she asks.

"Yeah."

We head to our next classes, and the end of the day seems to take forever, but I'm not in any hurry to get home.

The school bus pulls up to my stop. "See you later," Lily says, as I step off the bus. I walk home, hoping Rich's car is not in the driveway. It's empty, and I relax when I see Ginette standing on her porch, leaning over the railing. No Ferry.

"Hi, Ginette," I call. "Everything all right?"

"I haven't seen Ferry all day."

"He'll be back. Always is." I move to unlock my front door. But it isn't locked. Or closed. The door is slightly open. I step in and expect to see Mom smoking on the couch or lying on the bed in her bedroom, but I see Ferry. I can only recognize his grey stripes, but I know it's him. He's strung from the hook on the ceiling, where the fake flowers usually hang. He's tied by the tail. He's not moving. His eyes are open. His mouth is open. Empty. My stomach churns and rises into my throat. I swallow down burning bile. A bucket beneath him taps, collecting drops of blood. At the bottom of the bucket is a small pink blob. There's a note next to the bucket, in messy handwriting, and as I read it to myself, I hear Rich's gravelly voice: *Cat got your tongue?*

I scream. I think I scream. My throat is on fire, but I don't hear a sound. I run out of the house and sit in the melting mound of snow. I'm cold and wet, shivering and sick. I gag and heave into the snow, then cover up my vomit with ice. I'm crying. My nose is running.

My cheeks are burning. The crumpled note is still in my hand.

"You okay, girl?" Ginette calls to me. Everything is whipping by me, like I'm spinning on a carnival ride, dizzy and stuck in one spot. She stands up and waves at me, but I can't answer her. He may as well have cut out my tongue too. I try to catch my breath, but it comes out as sobs and heaves. Ginette is walking over. She's slow. I can't talk to her. I can't let her see Ferry. I close the door and run. I run out of the driveway. I run across the street. I hear Ginette yelling. A car honking. I stop and I'm in the middle of the road. The driver is yelling, waving their arms at me. I bend down, my elbows on my knees, and the driver is out of their car. They leave the door open.

"You all right?" they ask. It's woman in a chequered jacket. She pulls it tight around her. There is wind, but I don't feel it. I'm numb and cold and steaming hot.

"Sorry," I say and cross the street. I run up to *Le Dépanneur* and pull out my phone.

Chapter 11
Now Hiring

I dial Lily's number.

"You ready?" Lily answers. "We are gonna rock this science test."

"Can you . . ." I say, catching my breath, "come get me?"

"What's wrong?"

I don't want to keep this secret. I want to tell Lily and Ginette and everyone. The crumpled note falls from my hands. *Cat Got Your Tongue?* Stranger Danger Rich is going to chop me to pieces if I say a word.

"I'm okay," I lie.

"I'll ask Mom for the car,"

"Please," I whisper.

"On my way" Lily says and hangs up.

I call Mom. No answer. I try again. And again.

I text her:

Élise
Where are you?

Nothing. Ten minutes later Lily pulls up.

"What's going on?" Lily asks when I get into her car.

"Mom was upset with me for leaving again. No big deal. Can we stop at the grocery store first?"

"Sure," she says.

I need a plan.

- Get hold of Mom and figure out what the hell is happening (and make sure she's okay).

- Get pre-packaged food for lunches because I can't go back home.

- Find a place to sleep (a.k.a.: come clean to Lily).

I should tell Lily now. About Rich. And Ferry, but she'll freak out and probably want to call the cops or something.

We pull up to the store, the parking lot almost empty. "Should I come in or wait here?" she asks.

"Wait here."

I walk in and go straight to the canned goods. I get a bunch of dry noodle soups. Anything I can add water to and heat up in a microwave at school. I pick up some cans of tuna. And then I break. I drop my basket. The contents roll across the laminate floor. A clerk sees me and approaches, half running.

"Let me help you with that," he says.

"No!" I yell. "Sorry. I mean, thanks. I'm fine." He hands me a can of tuna from the floor. I shake my head. "I changed my mind. I don't want it." He places it back on the shelf.

"Are you all right?" he asks.

I see myself the way he might see me. I relax. I breathe. "Yeah. Just in a rush." I open my wallet to see if I have enough money to buy everything in my basket. "I'll be fine," I call to the clerk as I head to the junk food aisle. I get a bag of chips and candy for our study session.

At the register I wait for the cashier to scan all my food. She looks about my age, maybe older. Behind her is a bulletin board with announcements, including a *We're hiring* sign.

"Hi there," she says, noticing me looking at the sign. "Thinking of applying?"

"Oh. Not really."

"I'll take that, then." She takes my basket and starts scanning the items. "Forty-five and seventy," she says, and I look at the register. Then at my wallet. I hand her a fifty and she makes change.

"On second thought, how do I apply?" I ask.

She reaches behind her register and hands me a sheet of paper. "Here. Fill this out. Bring it to the manager." She points to the door near the exit that reads *Manager.* I pay for the food and stuff it in my school bag. I step aside and fill out the application near the exit, then knock on the office door.

"Yeah?" comes a rusty, scratchy voice from behind the door. "Come in."

The manager is a woman with greying hair. She's thin. Wrinkly.

"Hi. I'm here to give you this." I hand her the application. I hold my grocery bag in the other hand, and my arm is shaking from the weight, the exhaustion, and the stress, but I have to hold it together another few minutes.

She coughs into her elbow. It's a smoker's cough. Loud and rumbling. "Sorry about that," she says and takes my application.

"Élise?"

"Yes?"

"Can you start next Thursday?"

"Yeah. Okay."

"When does school let out?"

"Three-thirty."

"Great. You'll do four-thirty to nine Thursday and Friday. Weekends?"

"Sure." Whatever the hell gets me out of the house.

"Nine to five. You'll be bagging groceries. Helping clients to their cars. Stocking shelves. You strong? There's some heavy lifting involved."

I think about it. My arm is shaking. "Yeah, I'm strong."

"Good. I'll give you your training Thursday. Four thirty?"

"Thanks."

"See you then."

I leave the grocery store and find Lily waiting in her car. "That took a minute," she says. I place my bag in the back seat. "Tell me you at least got study snacks."

"And a job."

"Seriously?"

"I need cash."

"For college?" she asks.

"For everything," I say.

She wraps her arms around my shoulders as I'm placing my grocery bag in the back seat. She takes me by surprise and I almost fall on top of her. "You have to apply."

"I will. I'm sorry I blew off Mr. Hanes today. Anxious, you know. But I'll meet him Monday. Promise. I need to get the hell out of this town." I want to tell her why. I want to tell her, but she'll want to know everything, and I can't think of it now or I might completely fall apart. Right now all I can handle is candy and a science test I'll probably fail. "Can I sleep over tonight?"

"For sure. Is it okay with your mom, though? She was already upset you were leaving to study."

"It'll be fine," I say.

"Élise?"

"Yeah?"

"You can tell me anything. Like what's going on with your mom, or if you're worried about stuff. You can tell me."

"I know."

"I won't tell anyone. I mean, I can keep secrets."

"I know." And it's true. I trust her, completely, like a sister, but some secrets are too hard to tell.

My phone buzzes in my back pocket and I read Mom's text:

Mom
Home now. What the fuck?

Élise
Sleeping at Lily's tonight.

I know Mom is alive, and that's enough for now. I turn off my phone. My hands are shaking. Lily is driving, but she notices.

"Hey, you okay?" She places a hand on mine. I nod. I hold back the stinging in my eyes and my throat.

"No, but is it okay if we don't talk about it now?" is all I can say.

"Yeah. I guess," Lily says, and we're quiet the rest of the way to her house.

Chapter 12

Withdrawal

Lily's mom is great. She lets us study in Lily's room with loads of junk food. I have no appetite but force down a few pieces of candy so Lily doesn't think I'm sick. Her mom usually leaves us alone and never knocks on the door. Unless it's an emergency. Like when we hear Mom's voice in Lily's entrance, panting, shaking, calling my name, sharp and loud. "Élise!" Mom bursts into Lily's room. She has blood on her shirt. She's limping. Her leg is hurting her.

"Mom, what the hell?"

"Let's go. Now," she says.

Lily looks like she's watching a horror movie: my life.

"We're studying," I say.

"You're done. I said *now*."

"Claire, maybe we can calm down?" Lily's mom says. "Let Élise pack her things, then she'll come home with you."

Mom ignores Mrs. McLeod and talks straight at me. "Taxi is downstairs."

"I can drive you home," Mrs. McLeod says. Mom turns to her, like she's only just realized she's there, and hesitates. Her chest rises and falls, like she's been running. "Pay the driver and I'll drive you home when Élise is ready." Mom looks like she might pass out.

Mom shakes her head. "Now," she repeats. I pack up my books, fast. *Don't cry*, I tell myself. I leave without saying goodbye. Lily hasn't moved or changed expression. Mom grabs my hand and drags me out the door. She wasn't lying about the taxi, and I'm relieved it's not Rich's car idling in the driveway. She says nothing on the drive home. She pays the driver. She unlocks our side door and slams it shut after I walk in.

Ferry is gone. A spot of blood stains the floor.

"What the fuck happened?" Mom cries. "I came home and the cat . . . it was . . ." She's crying. For Ferry?

"I know."

"You know. You fucking left it there for me to find?"

"I thought . . . I thought you left it there for me to find," I say.

I dare to look at Mom. Her hair is grey and probably hasn't been washed in a week. Her tie dye T-shirt is spotted with blood. She's sweaty. She's scared.

"You think I would do this? It's fucking disgusting."

"You let a psycho drug dealer into our home. I guess he found a way in."

"Rich?"

"Yeah. The guy has been following me around. Knows

who my friends are."

"What did he say to you?"

"To shut up about him being here. About you two . . ." The chips and candy from my study session with Lily threaten to make an appearance. I swallow them down.

"Asshole. I'll take care of it," Mom says.

"What will you do?"

"You don't need to worry about it."

"Our cat . . ." I start, but I can't get through it without choking. "Ferry was strung up in our living room, Mom. Nothing you do can take it away."

"Why would he do that? Who would you tell?"

"He saw my agenda. I was supposed to have an appointment with the guidance counsellor today."

"Shit, Élise."

"I didn't meet with him. Rich found me at the bus stop. Told me not to say anything about him. Then when I came home . . . and he left a note."

I tell Mom what it said. Mom exhales. She paces through her puff of smoke, which dispels into the room like a ghost. "Maybe you should go back to Lily's house."

"What are you going to do?" I ask.

"It's safer for you there."

"Why'd you come get me, then?"

"I don't know, okay? I panicked." She's shaking. Her eyes are glassy. Her whole body is rigid, like she's in pain. She cups her head in her hand. "Fucking migraine coming," she says. She goes into her room and pops open a pill bottle. "Fuck!" she says and throws the empty bottle across the living room. She opens a drawer, searching for the bottle Rich brought her. "Shit," she says. "They're gone. They're all gone. He took them." She comes back out and leans on the kitchen table, holding her stomach.

"What is it?" I ask.

"Cramps."

This day is the equivalent to the leftover cruddy food in the sink, stuck to the drain stopper after you wash the dishes. And now Mom is going through withdrawal. My phone vibrates with a text from Lily.

Lily
Are u ok? Mom ok?

Mom sees me reading the text. "It's Lily," I say.

"Ask her to get you," Mom says. She grunts with pain. She's sweaty but has goosebumps on her arms.

"I can't leave you alone like this."

"Get me some Advil." I rummage through the medicine cabinet in the bathroom and find a bottle of Advil gel caps. I hand it to her. She opens it and takes four.

"Jesus, Mom, take it easy."

"It's fine. Call your friend."

I text Lily:

Élise
Can you come back for me?

Lily
Be there in ten.

By the time Lily arrives, Mom has crawled her way into bed. She's still moaning with pain, but it's muffled into her pillow.

"You sure you want me to leave?" I call out to her.

I hear her gag and heave and vomit. I'm about to turn her doorknob but she yells, "Go!" as Lily's headlights streak through the window. I don't want to leave Mom alone, but I can't let Lily in to see her like this either. I'm about to step outside but stop. I open my bag. I leave four cans of beef stew on the counter. Ms. McLeod is driving. I plop down into the backseat next to Lily. We don't drive off right away.

"We can go," I say.

"I need to go."

Chapter 13
Hugs Instead of Slamming Doors

When I climb into the back seat, Lily is there, her arm clutching the headrest. I sit next to her. Her arm wraps around my shoulder, and hugs me close. She has no clue what's happened today, or how much I need her to hold me right now. I don't tell myself not to cry. I let it all pour out on her shoulder, and she doesn't ask me a single thing.

★ ★ ★

The next morning is awkward. I wake up before Lily, and her mom is already in the kitchen, making coffee. She hears me stirring and waves me over to the kitchen table. She puts a mug in front of me and is about to pour. I never drink coffee. I shake my head, and she passes the milk instead. I pour it into my mug.

"Sleep okay?" Mrs. McLeod asks.

"Yeah. Thanks." I sip my milk.

"Lily says you've been hesitating about your application? For college?"

I sigh. I want to drink my milk in silence.

"I'm meeting with Mr. Hanes on Monday. I'll get it sorted out."

"You can stay the weekend," Lily's mom says. "Longer, too, if you need. I don't want you to worry about food or a place to study. You're welcome here. Anytime."

"Thanks. I should get back home, though."

"You have a bag filled with groceries in the entrance. Do you need to take them to your mom? I can drop them off today."

"No. They're mine. I mean . . . I left her some food."

"I mean it, Élise. You can stay. If for no other reason than my girls actually get along when you're around." She flashes a weak smile. "I like having you here."

My arms tingle. I feel weak, but I sit up. "Thanks. I'll . . . I'll see how it goes," is all I say. When I walk back into Lily's room, she's sitting up in her bed. I roll up the sleeping bag on the floor between her bed and Tamara's. Tamara is still asleep, snoring quietly, holding onto a stuffed penguin.

"You okay?" Lily asks.

"Fine," I say. "My bike is still here, so I think I'll ride home."

"You don't have to go so early," she says. "Stay the day. Maybe tomorrow too. We can . . . figure things out."

"I want to make sure Mom's all right."

"I know. But then you can come back." Lily runs a hand through her wildly curly hair. "I want you to be safe."

"I know." I don't look at her. If I do, I'll start crying again.

Lily stands and heads to the bathroom. I pack up the rest of my things, including my grocery bag, and change back into my clothes.

I can overhear Lily and her mom in the living room.

"When she's ready," her mom says.

"I'm scared for her," Lily says. "And I don't get what's happening."

"Wait. Listen. She'll tell you."

Lily walks back into the bedroom, where I'm zipping up my bag.

"I can drive you," Lily says.

"Lily, all this stuff, with my mom, it's . . ."

"It's okay."

"Saying it out loud, it's terrifying."

"I won't tell anyone."

"I know. I trust you. But . . ."

"But what?"

"I feel like something bad will happen."

"Something bad *is* happening. Your mom showed up with blood on her shirt, all crazy, and took you away, then sent you back half an hour later."

"I'm sorry."

"You don't have to apologize. But . . . let me in on what's happening. So I can help."

"You *are* helping." Lily puts her hand on mine, stopping me from tying up the sleeping bag. I want her help, and I want her to be here for me, but I don't want to talk about everything, and if I do, it will be on my terms. She might turn and run from me when she hears the story of last night, and I can't bear that. I'm better off dealing with this my own way. "I don't need the constant nagging. Not about my application or about field trips, or about my mom." The dread and regret boil inside me before I finish what I'm saying, knowing it's totally unfair to Lily.

"Nagging? It's called caring. You know, worrying about you."

"It's a bit much sometimes."

"A bit much? I want you to be safe and go to college."

"I get it, but it's all you ever talk about. College might make sense for you, but my life is a disaster. Leaving for college is not going to help."

"You said you wanted to leave this town. You said you wanted to go."

"I do. But I can't."

"I need you there," Lily says. She's been kind. And patient. Helpful and caring, but now it's like all this talk of college, it's for her sake, not mine.

"You need me there because you know you're too scared to go on your own." I may as well have slapped her in the face. Her eyes water. Her cheeks are red. Her whole face is on fire.

"Maybe you should go," Lily says. Tamara rolls over in her bed. Her eyes open.

"Hey, Élise," she says, her voice little and sleepy.

"See you Monday," I say to Lily and haul my bag over my shoulder.

I plough my bike through the slush out of their driveway, but Mrs. McLeod is out in her slippers calling after me. She looks crazy, but then again, it's nothing compared to Mom.

"Élise, wait!" she calls out, tightening her robe and cinching the belt around her.

"I have to go," I say. I place my foot on the pedal. Mrs. McLeod is out in the snow in fluffy pink slippers, hanging onto my handlebars.

"Please, stay."

"I should check on Mom," I say.

"We will. Together. Later. I don't want you going alone." Her eyes are wide and watery. She's scared. For me. "I know you're worried about her. So am I, but your safety is my priority. I can't let you go. Please, stay." She sounds desperate.

"Lily and I had an argument."

"So we'll work it out. You two are best friends. She cares about you and . . . well, you need us." Mrs. McLeod has a way of being blunt but kind. And she's a hundred percent right. "Call your mom, but stay here today. Please."

"What if she comes to get me again?"

"I'll find a way to keep you here."

"Please don't call the police," I say and surprise myself at how terrified I sound. I think of Mom how she used to be. When I was little, she'd always let me do stuff on my own. School projects, the dishes, placing the eggs in a bag at the grocery store. She let me figure it out and make a mess sometimes, but she never got mad. *You crack some eggs, you clean it up,* she'd say. *You'll figure it out.* And most of the time, I did. I liked that she let me. It made me feel grown up. But now, all I want is for someone to clean up my mess and show me what to do. Mrs. McLeod and Lily are trying.

I have to let them. "I know last night was crazy, but she wasn't going to hurt me or anything. She was worried about me and panicked. I don't want her to get in trouble."

I feel like a three-year-old when Lily's mom places her hand on mine. "I want to keep you safe. I don't want her in trouble either."

I take it as a promise, even though I know Mrs. McLeod is a responsible adult, and if Mom shows up again, bloody and raging, there is no way the cops won't be involved. I go back inside and text Mom:

Élise
Staying at Lily's today. Please don't come without calling first. Are you ok?

Lily is in the kitchen with Tamara. She's serving her sister some milk, and it's the first time I've seen them together not arguing. It looks like Lily's been crying.

"I'm sorry," she says when I walk in.

"I was being an asshole," I say. "Shit, sorry," I blurt out, holding my hand in front of my mouth. Tamara smiles.

"So was I," Lily says. "You're right. I've been nagging. I'll give you space. I promise. Stay. Please." She looks like her mom.

"I'll stay."

She stands and hugs me. We hug a lot, but this catches me off guard. I'm not used to arguments ending in hugs instead of slammed doors.

Chapter 14

Getting Help

Mom doesn't text me back all Saturday, and I finally get sign of life from her on Sunday morning.

Mom
I'm ok. Come home after school tomorrow.

I'm not sure I want to go back. Lily's mom says it's up to me, but she wants me to stay with them. I focus on studying for Science and meeting with Mr. Hanes.

The next day when I arrive at his office, he's standing in the doorframe, smiling. I walk in.

"Glad you could make it," he says.

"Sorry about Friday."

"No problem. You're here now. Tell me about the college visit. Anything pique your interest?" His cheeriness is genuine. It's a great distraction from the weekend.

"It was interesting."

"Okay. Good. Anywhere you're considering applying?"

Flashback to Mom, doubled over on her bed, groaning with pain.

"No."

"Why not?"

The sound of her vomiting into a bucket on her bedroom floor.

"It's not about school. I think I'd like it. Especially being in the city. With Lily. But, leaving home it's complicated."

Mom's hand around my neck. Her snarl. Stranger Danger in my kitchen. I have every reason to want to leave.

"I get your mom is having trouble recuperating from her accident. But she can get help. Whatever you think she needs, we can find a solution. Keeping you out of school isn't possibly going to help her."

"Good point."

"It's about money?"

"Yeah."

"I understand your mom is on disability? Welfare? Having a child in her care means she will receive more funds?" He actually gets it. "Many students feel the same pressure to stay home after high school. They almost all regret their choice."

"How do I help her, then?"

"How we help depends on what she needs."

"She hasn't had a job since the accident." Mom's hand tightens. I try to breathe.

"Where did she work before?" he asks.

"All over. The tire factory. A few gas stations. Canadian Tire. But now, she takes medication and it makes her . . . forgetful."

"Forgetful how? She doesn't know what day it is? Where she is?"

"No. Forgetful, lazy. Like she won't get food, even if she has the money."

"Do you often lack money for food?"

"It runs out."

"Quickly?"

"Sometimes."

"Do you know what medication she's taking?"

"For her leg. And her back. For the pain," I add, but I know that's not why she still takes them. The lie weighs me down. I want to answer his questions honestly. "I think she's addicted to them." Mom squeezes harder. My neck, my throat. She cuts off my airway. "When she doesn't have them, it's like she's sick." He nods. Doesn't say anything. Doesn't ask another question.

Finally, he says, "Tell me about it."

I rub my throat. Mr. Hanes moves my hand away. My eyes sting. My throat is dry and I cough. "Élise?" I look up at him. "I'm here to listen. If I think you need help, then I'll help."

"She's my mom. She's a total wreck. But I can't leave her."

"What I'm hearing you say is, you love your mom, you're afraid and you want to protect her, but you want what's best for yourself too."

"You a mind reader?"

"I've been doing this a long time. And I'll be honest with

you. The drug use. The lack of food . . ." I'm crying now. No tears, but my insides are burning with the effort to keep them in. I keep the tears down, but the dam breaks and I tell him. I tell him about Stranger Danger following me to the bus stop, and I tell him about Ferry and last night.

"This guy, Rich, is supplying her with the pills?"

I nod.

"How is she paying him?" My eyes well up. I remember him in his boxers, closing her bedroom door, the noises I had to drown out. "Any way she can?"

"Yeah."

"Is Rich the only man who has been to your place?"

"That I know of. You think there might be more?"

"I think someone like Rich could take advantage of your mom's addiction and use her to make a profit. With other men."

"Like a pimp?" Mr. Hanes taps his pencil on his desk, as the thought sinks in. It's clear Mom wasn't sleeping with him because she likes him. The way she was pushing him out the door that morning — she didn't want him there. "Ferry wasn't only a warning to me. It was to Mom too."

"Makes sense," Mr. Hanes says.

"Shit," I say. "It's so fucked up."

"Why?"

"Because I still don't want to leave her. She's still my mom and she was a good one before the accident. Sometimes she still is. She still tries to protect me, but it's like everything is in a mist, a fog, you know, that she can't find her way out of."

"I'm going to make a call."

"The police?" I say, terrified.

"Child protection."

Oh.

"Will someone come take me away?"

"No. Someone will come to check up on your mom. They'll call first. If she refuses, they might find foster care for you. If she complies, a social worker from child protection will come. They'll make an assessment. They'll make a recommendation for resources for you and your mom. Foster care is part of the process, but not always. Not if your mom accepts help, follows through."

"What if I don't want you to call?"

"It gives me more reason to think I need to, but I have an obligation to call either way."

"Don't tell Lily."

"This is all confidential." I relax. A little. "But she is your best friend, and a good one to have. If you need a safe place to stay, I think she and her family are people you can count on. Right?"

"Yeah."

"She'll understand. More than you think."

"When will you call?"

"After you leave my office. I can call with you here, if you like."

"No!" I clear my throat. "Please, no." We sit in silence while a minute ticks on the clock. I need a distraction. "Mr. Hanes?"

"Yeah."

"Can we look at filling out an application anyway?"

"You bet."

Chapter 15
Application

I tell Mr. Hanes about the ALC program at Dawson. He agrees it would be a good choice, and sticking with Lily would be smart. We fill out the application together. It's easy, like Lily said, until we get to the point where I have to pay a thirty-dollar fee. I stop to explain, but Mr. Hanes pulls out his bank card from his wallet and fills in the number to pay.

"What are you doing?" I ask.

"No worries, Élise."

"You're going to pay for my application? I got a job, I can pay you back."

"My gift. Because you've worked so hard. You deserve it."

"I'll pay you back," I say again. He waves me off and fills the information in on his computer.

"Are there other kids . . . who can't pay the fee? Or who couldn't afford the field trip?" He seems surprised by my question. "You said other students have similar difficulties. As me. At home."

"There are a few."

"Did you pay for them, too?"

He leans back in his chair. Crosses his arms. "Yeah. With pleasure."

"Can't there be another way to get us to apply to college without you dishing out the cash for everyone?"

"What do you mean?" he asks.

"Like a fund or something. By the school. To help kids out, so we don't feel so . . . pitiful taking your money."

"You feel ashamed?"

"It's kind of embarrassing."

"And if the money came from a school fund, you'd feel better about it?"

"I'd know I wasn't the only kid in the same situation. It would help a bit. Or get me to ask for help if I knew it existed."

"Good point. Maybe you should bring it up."

"To who?"

"Start with your Leadership teacher. I think he would be impressed with the idea. If you come up with a plan, you could take it to the principal and start up a fund, like you said."

"You think it would work?"

"It's a great idea. I think you can make it happen. This is why you deserve college. All those ideas in here." He leans forward and taps me on the head with his pencil.

"You're still going to call child protection?"

The air stills. He looks at me over his thick glasses. "I have to."

"When will they come?"

"They'll call first. Within the next twenty-four hours."

"Okay. Thanks, Mr. Hanes."

"You bet," he says. I stand to leave. When I open the door, Lily is texting, waiting for me.

"How'd it go?" she asks.

"She did it," Mr. Hanes says. He nods to Lily, who's beaming. "See you soon," he says to me. Lily and I make our way to the cafeteria.

"ALC at Dawson?" she asks.

The tears are still stinging, behind everything. I nod. "Thanks, Lily. You're the best."

"Imagine us, together at college."

"If they accept me."

"They will. It's going to be amazing."

I think so, too, but first I have to get through the next twenty-four hours.

Chapter 16
First Shift

It's Tuesday and still no phone call. I walk on eggshells around Mom, when she's awake. I know when she runs out of pills, she gets grouchy, but the other day with Rich, that was the first time she was aggressive. She's calmer today than the night she came to get me at Lily's. I peek into her room when she's outside smoking. The pill bottle on her night stand isn't full, but it's not empty, either, which means she's seen Rich in the last twenty-four hours. Even though . . . Ferry. My skin crawls thinking he may have been over here while I was at school. I feel him here. His smell and his gravelly voice are trapped in the smog of our house.

On Wednesday I'm sure the phone will ring, and Mom will turn on me when child protection tells her they're coming over, but they still don't call. Mr. Hanes said sometimes they get backed up or emergencies arise, and they have to deal with more urgent cases first. There are some worse off than me, I remind myself.

Thursday morning I hear a car pull up. It's early, before my alarm goes off. I hear Mom slam the screen door shut. Voices outside. Not loud, but not calm. Mom is asking Rich to leave. He wants to come inside. "Just for a little," he says. "She won't know I'm here. You owe me."

Mom says something I can't hear, then I hear him laugh. His gruff voice is loud and echoes into the silent morning. The car drives off. I wait twenty minutes before coming out of my room, ready for school. Mom is on the couch. No sign of Rich, but when I walk to the bus stop, I see his rusty little Toyota driving up the hill. He flashes his high beams but drives past me, and I watch him turn onto our street at the top of the hill.

My heart flips, thinking of Mom opening up the door for a cat-murdering drug dealer. On the bus, Lily is reviewing her science notes and we barely talk. The test is brutal. After school Mom is home alone, but Rich's stink is like a heavy cloud hovering in the living room. She's eating mac and cheese in silence.

I tell Mom I got a job and start today. She barely acknowledges me. She grunts. Her skin looks like there's a film on it, liquid or grease. It's greyish, and her eyes are like two beads surrounded by dark purple bags. I don't think she's been eating much, and probably smoking more. I bike to the grocery store after dropping off my school things at home.

No one has called. No one has come to visit, and I

haven't told Lily about any of it.

It's my first shift at the store, and I meet the manager who shows me how to bag groceries. Eggs and bread should always be placed on top. Heavy things on the bottom. Don't overpack the bags, and always offer to bring the client's groceries to their car. Easy. Except Thursday is when the week's specials come out, and it's crazy busy. I bag as quickly as I can without dropping anything. I feel like I'm on one of those game shows where contestants have to do some ridiculous task, and they're timed with an annoying buzzer. Instead of a buzzer, I have an old lady watching me bag her things, one hand on her hip, huffing and puffing. What can she possibly be in a rush for?

"Would you like me to take these to your car?"

"Well, I should hope so," she says.

I walk behind her in the parking lot, and she pops the trunk of a red Nissan. I gently place the bags in the car, so they won't move around too much while she drives. I'll bet she's a real speed demon. "All set," I say.

"Here you go." She holds out her hand. I open my palm, and she drops a two-dollar coin into it.

"Thanks," I say.

"Young people like you should work hard," she says, "and get paid for it."

"Thanks again." I close her trunk. Who would have thought?

The rest of the evening flies by, and I make about twenty dollars in tips. I see the manager after my shift and tell her about it. "It's all yours," she says. "You can expect to make good tips on Thursdays through the weekend. Tips aside, did everything go all right?"

"Yeah. I liked it. Kept me busy. Everyone here is nice. The clients too." Even impatient old ladies.

"Great. So I'll see you tomorrow?"

"Definitely. Thanks again."

I made twenty dollars, plus the salary the store will pay me. I'll be able to save up for an apartment in no time. I step out into the almost-spring chill, still windy and biting. But I leave my first shift feeling more hopeful than I have in months.

Then all my hope turns to cold dread when a blue Toyota drives up to the entrance of the grocery store.

Chapter 17
Fear, Strength, and Kindness

The spokes of my bike *click-click* as I walk it through the parking lot. The Toyota follows. I feel like fainting or throwing up, but I can't look afraid. Rich rolls down his window.

"Hey, kitty cat," he says. "Nice uniform." I'm still wearing the green apron with the store logo on it under my coat. "Need a lift?"

"Actually, my boss is going to give me a lift home."

"With the bike?"

"Yeah, I was just about to put it into her truck." I point my chin in the direction of a white pickup, hoping no one comes and drives off in it. When Rich turns to look behind him at the truck, I head back to the entrance, but he calls out to me.

"Your mom told me to pick you up." He's lying. No

way is he here to take me home.

"I'll be home soon!" I yell. But then he's out of his car, his hand around my wrist. I drop my bike. There are only a few cars in the lot and no one is outside. "Let go of me!" I yell, straining against his grasp.

"We had a deal." He's starting to pull me toward his car.

"Let go!" I say, louder.

"You snitched, and now someone from child protection was knocking on the door," he whispers, beer breath blowing in my face.

I stop struggling. Mom. Child protection is there now. If Rich knows this, then Mom definitely let him into the house. I'm angry and afraid and it's too much emotion to hold back. I pull away from Rich as hard as I can, but he squeezes my wrist tighter.

"Élise?" A boy named James who trained with me today is at the entrance to the store. "Élise, that you?"

"Shit," Stranger Danger says.

"You okay?" James jogs right up to me and Rich.

"See you, kid," Rich says, and gets into his car, then drives off.

James picks up my bike and stands next to me. He's a year younger but about a foot taller. I think I feel his hand on my shoulder. "Élise? You okay?" he repeats.

"I have to get home," I say.

"I can drive you, but, um, maybe you should call someone? We could go back inside?"

"Good idea," I say and head back into the store. James walks my bike for me. "I'll be fine. You can go." I met James a few hours ago and don't need to fill him in on all

95

the drama surrounding my so-called life. He gets in his car and leaves, as I take my bike and walk through the automatic doors.

"Élise. You're still here? We're about to close up. Everything all right?" my manager asks.

"Someone is coming to pick me up, but is it okay if I wait inside?"

She looks me up and down. I must look pale and terrified. "Of course. You sure you're all right?"

"Yeah. Thanks."

"You can wait in my office. And you can leave your bike here if you need to." She leaves and I call Lily.

"You done work?" Lily answers.

"Yeah. Do you think your mom can come pick me up?"

"What's wrong?"

I can't keep lying to her. "So much is so wrong, Lily, but can I tell you when we get to your place?"

"You want to sleep over?"

"Please."

"Of course. Um. Give us ten minutes?"

"Sure," I say.

She hangs up, but in a minute, my phone rings again. The ID says *Hanes, George*. Mr. Hanes.

"Hello?"

"Élise, are you home?"

"I'm at work."

"Good. Child protection called your mom. Repeatedly. She hadn't answered, so they arrived at your place about half an hour ago. She didn't take it too well. Since you weren't home, they called me to track you down. Are you safe?"

"I'm going to spend the night at Lily's."

"Good idea."

"Mr. Hanes?"

"Yeah?"

"Is Mom okay?"

"She didn't want to let them in when they arrived. She got aggressive. Started yelling."

"Are they still there now?"

"Child protection had to call the police," he says.

"Did they take her?" I ask.

"Yeah. To get her to calm down. I'll have more news soon. I'll call you as soon as I do."

I picture my mom yelling at the person from child protection, them forcing their way in. Seeing the empty fridge and pill bottles. Rich must have been there and bolted the second he realized what was happening, before the cops showed up.

"Someone is threatening me. And my mom."

There's a pause.

"Tell me about it," he says.

I check to see if anyone is hanging around outside the office door. There's no one. I tell him about Rich. About the cat. About him showing up tonight. "He might know where Lily lives. I think he's been following me."

"Does Lily know this?"

"No."

"Then you need to tell her. And her mom." He clears his throat. "And the police."

"What will happen to my mom?"

"They'll wait until she's calm to question her. If she complies, they'll release her. They'll give her options."

"Which are?"

"She'll have to follow through with therapy. Drug counselling. Family counselling. If she follows the recommendations, you can stay with her."

"And if she doesn't?"

"You'll have to go to court. Foster care, unless you have someone who can be a temporary guardian for you."

"Like Lily's mom?"

"If she agrees to it."

"I think she will. If I'm completely honest with her."

"Then I guess you have an important conversation to have tonight. Anything I can do to help?"

"No. It'll be all right."

"Be sure to make a police report about this Rich person. Tonight. Right away."

"Yeah."

"Élise?"

"Yeah?"

"You're a strong kid. But you can ask for help."

"I know. Thanks."

"Come and see me, first thing tomorrow morning. You, the principal, and I will have to sit down and talk about everything. I suggest you bring Lily with you, and I'll phone her mom tomorrow to fill everyone in on how to be most supportive for you."

I don't know what to say. It's completely overwhelming to know all these people need to meet to discuss my messed-up life. There's a knock at the door, and the manager pokes her head in. "Élise, your lift is here. Someone named Lily?"

"Coming. Mr. Hanes, gotta go."

"Okay. You have my number."

"Thanks. For everything."

I meet Lily in the front of the store, and she wraps her arms around me in a hug. It's warm and strong and filled with fear. Her mom is standing next to her car in the parking lot, and she hugs me too. Like they don't know what's going on, and it doesn't matter. They don't know what happened, but they know they want to help. It's kindness I've never had before.

Chapter 18
The Truth

The car ride is quiet, but when we get to Lily's house, I tell them everything. The drugs. Rich. The cat. Child protection and the police.

Lily's mom doesn't miss a beat. She calls the cops and asks to fill out a report about Rich. An hour later they're at the front door, asking me all kinds of questions. They write everything down. I describe him, his car, what I think he was doing with my mom. It's embarrassing. Lily's mom makes us all tea. I'm sure she has a ton of her own questions, but she lets me talk without interruption. I'm so used to Mom cutting me off anytime I try to talk to her, but Mrs. McLeod, Mr. Hanes, and the police all give me space to find my words, because saying all this out loud takes time.

For the first time, I tell everyone the whole truth. When I'm done, the police tell me Rich is no stranger to them. A known drug dealer. Harassing a minor and killing an animal might lead to an arrest. I ask about my mom, but they don't have an update on her. They take my number and promise to get in touch when they know more. It's close to midnight when they leave.

Lily's mom pours more tea for herself and offers me more, but I feel like I've been up all night, running a marathon. My head is pounding, and I want sleep. But I need to ask her something first.

"Mrs. McLeod?"

"Yeah?"

"If Mom doesn't agree to therapy — if they say she can't take care of me . . ."

"You don't need to ask, Élise." She places a perfectly manicured hand over mine. "Of course you can stay with us." Her eyes well up. "You can stay as long as you need."

"I might have to go to court."

"Then I'll come with you."

"Mr. Hanes wants to meet tomorrow. With you, the principal, and me. Can you come?"

"Of course."

My body is like a rubber band, finally released from holding together some huge package. I get to be me, without bracing myself for the next thing. Lily doesn't say much. She's been wiping away tears, listening to my story. She links arms with me and leads me to her room. I usually sleep on the floor between her and Tamara's beds. "Want to sleep in the bed?" she offers.

I nod. "Can you stay with me?"

Exhausted, we crawl under her covers. We lie side by side, facing each other.

"I'm sorry we fought," she says.

"It's okay."

"It's not. I was mean. And a little selfish. I didn't understand what was happening and why you wouldn't tell me."

"It was hard to believe everything that was happening," I say. "I wasn't too nice either. I know you'd be fully capable of going to college on your own, and you'll be amazing."

"You were right, though. I do need you," Lily says.

"Me too."

We laugh through tears neither of us is afraid to show.

"Thanks for nagging me. And not giving up on me."

"That's what sisters do," Lily says. "They fight, and they love each other." She points to Tamara snoring in her bed. "I should know."

We fall asleep, our hands linked together.

Sleep comes easily, for once.

Chapter 19
Safety

I wake up before Lily and her mom. I make coffee. I don't usually drink it, but it's the least I can do for her mom this morning. School is going to be torture today, but I guess I'll be excused from some classes to meet with Mr. Hanes.

"Morning," Lily's mom greets me when the coffee is done brewing.

"Hi."

"How'd you sleep?"

"Surprisingly well," I say.

"Do you need to pass by home to pick up anything before school?"

I almost forgot my books are still at home. And I'll need to pack some clean clothes. I check my phone, but there are no texts from Mom or the police. My guess is she's still in custody. I try calling her anyway. No answer. Which means she's either still with the police, or she's passed out at home.

"I guess we'll need to pass by."

"I'll be with you," she says. It's more comfort than she knows.

When we pull up in the driveway, Ginette is on her porch, smoking. She stands when she sees us.

"Girl, where have you been? It's been a nightmare . . ."

"Hi, Ginette. Do you know if my mom is back?"

"Don't think so. You know the police picked her up last night?"

"Yeah. Long story."

"You okay, girl?"

"Staying with a friend. I'll be all right. Came to get stuff. Can you do me a favour?"

"Sure thing."

"If Mom comes home, tell her I'm all right. She can call me. I want to see her."

"You bet. You're going to be safe?"

"Yes."

"Haven't seen Ferry in a long time now," Ginette says.

"I know. I don't think he'll be back."

"It was about time he found his way out of here anyway. Probably off catching mice and charming some felines."

"He's quite the charmer," I say. My key sticks in the lock. I picture Ferry curling himself around my leg, purring, as I try to open the door. Sometimes he'd sneak right past me the second I got the door open. He'd bolt straight into the house and jump up on the counter, then meow at the cupboard. I'd pet him and open a can of food for him, and we'd sit on the couch or on my bed until he was ready to go outside for the night. He didn't come by every day, so when he did, it was like a friend popping in to say hi. I'd make time for him, no matter what was going on. It was like he was making time for me out of his busy alley cat schedule too.

Lily walks in after me and the screen door slams behind her, snapping me out of my thoughts of Ferry. Lily's mom enters too.

"Oh my god," Lily says.

The place is a disaster. There's stuff everywhere, like a burglar came in, threw everything around, then locked the door behind them. I understand what Mr. Hanes meant when he said Mom was aggressive. I picture her throwing things, trashing the place. I go to my room to collect my things, hoping I won't find everything thrown around like in the rest of the house. Nothing has been touched. Except my sketchpad. It's open on my bed, but I know I left it in my bag yesterday. It's open to my drawing of Mom on the couch, smoking. She's beautiful. She's sad and beautiful.

"Need help with anything?" Lily asks.

"There's a duffel bag in the closet. Dump everything from my drawers in it."

Lily packs up my clothes.

All my school stuff is accounted for.

"Got everything?" Lily's mom asks.

"Yeah." I tear out the picture from my sketchbook. I want to write Mom a letter about how even though she's a total mess, I love her and want her to be better, but I can't find the words for it, so I leave the sketch on the counter for her to find. Hopefully she'll understand this is how I want to see her.

★ ★ ★

We meet in Mr. Hanes's office. Me, Lily, her mom, the social worker from child protection, the principal, and a police officer. All because of me. They kept Mom in custody overnight, but she'll be released today. A court date will be set to determine if I continue to live with her or go to foster care. In the meantime, Lily's mom has to apply to the court to be my guardian. Child protection will have regular check-ins with my mom. I am allowed to visit her when I want, with supervision from the social worker.

Mom is expected to follow through with drug counselling. The officer says she seemed compliant last night once she'd calmed down. Compliant enough to also make a complaint about Rich. She knew where to find him, and he is now in custody. My rubber-band tension releases again. Everything is still such a mess, but at least now I know what's next.

The officer and social worker leave. Lily's mom heads off to work. The principal goes back to her office. Lily and I stay with Mr. Hanes.

"This is all good, right, Élise?" Mr. Hanes says.

"It is."

"How do you feel about the arrangement?"

"Good. But what if Mom follows all the recommendations? And the court decides I can live with her again?

What if I still want to stay with Lily's mom, until I leave for college?"

"It's up to you."

"Mom can't force me to live with her?"

"You're sixteen. You've suffered trauma with her. You're on your way to college. I doubt the court would force you back."

"You think I'll get accepted into the program?"

"Definitely," he says, sticking a pencil behind his ear and leaning back in his chair.

"She's a shitty mom," I say. "But I love her." And I realize, even with everything Mom has done, it's true. I do really love her. Because before there was an accident, too many pills, and a creepy pimp guy, we were barely scraping by. But we were a team. It's only since the accident I've felt like I've been carrying our team alone. But maybe Mom feels the same way. I don't know what the solution will be, and it's not easy to trust a bunch of strangers, but right now, I have to.

"Of course you love her," Mr. Hanes says. "I'm proud of you for making your own decision to be safe and happy. It's not easy."

I shake my head.

"So, what's next?" he asks. "I hear there's a math test to worry about?"

I groan.

"Yeah. We should cram," Lily says.

"First, I want to talk to the principal," I say.

"What about?" Lily asks.

"My idea about the fund. What do you think, Mr. Hanes?"

"I think it's a worthy idea. But the end of the year is fast approaching. You need to focus on your studies. Make sure you graduate. I don't know that you have the time to give to a commitment like starting up a fund."

"Oh."

"Don't get me wrong. The school needs it. The students need it. But now, my concern is you. You need to make sure you pass all your exams."

"He's right," Lily adds.

"Propose the idea to the Leadership teacher. To next year's students. Maybe draw up a quick outline of what you think the needs are. And let them build something from it."

"Okay. It's just . . . I wanted to be involved."

"Commit your time to yourself right now, Élise. You deserve that." I know he's right.

"You got a job too," Lily reminds me. "And you need it. That'll take up time."

"Okay. I'll talk to our Leadership teacher about it. See what he thinks," I say.

"He'll love the idea, I'm sure," Mr. Hanes says.

"Thank you. For everything," I tell Mr. Hanes.

"Anytime," he says. "So, we've sent off the applications. Now we wait. And work. Keep working hard."

"I will," I say.

"We should start with studying math." Says Lilly.

We head to the library to study. Trigonometry. Not exactly my specialty, but it makes me think of J.T. I pull the card out of my wallet.

"What's that?" Lily asks.

"J.T. from Dawson gave it to me. She works in student

services. She said she could help us find jobs and an apartment. She left me her number."

"You want to text her?"

"I think so. Just to tell her we both applied. That maybe she should look out for us in September or something."

"Yeah. Okay. Then we study."

I pull out my phone and text J.T.:

Élise

Hi. Élise from Joliette. The artist? Thought I'd let you know, I applied to Dawson! Hope to see you in September.

Lily watches me while she opens up her math notes. A minute later my phone buzzes with a text from J.T.:

J.T.

Awesome! Let me know when you get your acceptance. We'll talk about getting you set up.

She includes a crossed-fingers emoji.

"What's that face?" Lily says. "You keeping secrets from me?"

"No. This is my happy face." I stick out my tongue. "Can't you tell?" I show her the text and open up my books. For the next half hour, Lily quizzes me on right angles and formulas. And I don't even dread taking the test. Not if it gets me one step closer to where I need to be.

"Ready?" Lily asks, a minute before the bell rings for Math class.

"Ready," I say.

Acknowledgements

Every seed of an idea needs all the right stuff to flourish. Thank you to the following people for giving me every opportunity to complete this book.

To my parents, Pietro Beddia and Anna Manno, who have always held me up, supported me, and cheered me on. They never put themselves first. I am so lucky to have you.

To my husband Sébastien, dad extraordinaire, for giving me time and space to write, while entertaining our three children.

To my siblings Frank, Josie, and Cathy Beddia, who always looked out for me when I was younger and who today are my loudest cheerleaders: I love you.

Allister Thompson, editor. Your kindness and encouragement are so greatly appreciated. Thank you for rooting for me from the start and for helping me get this off the ground.